MILLION DOLLAR DREAM

To: Keisha From: Trainer Dee ♡

DERRICK FELDER

Million Dollar Dream
Derrick Felder

© 2016 Derrick Felder

ISBN- 13: 978-1519360465

ISBN- 10: 1519360460

Published by Broken Bars Publishing

www.brokenbarspublishing.com

Printed in the United States of America

Dedication

This dedication is designed to acknowledge all who've helped, supported and encouraged me to write and share this novel with the public. If I've missed anyone, blame it on my mind, not my heart.

Family:

My son Nadir Muhammed Felder 1/12/15-3/13/15. Mom, for keeping the original manuscript intact for me. Dad, my sister Sherina, my Brother Troy (my biggest fan and supporter), my uncle Tone (my Rock), my Grandparents, Devin, aunt Joy, Shantà, Ashley, Uncle Jack, and Brian.

Close friends and supporters:

Samir, Boop, Jabari, Malik, Harun, Ishmael, Bilal (Oliver Hudson) Bilal (Boob) Black, KB, Kanae, Rahman, Flizz, Petey, Corey, Ceez, EG1, Kacy, Keylan, Dana, for helping me put this novel onto a flash drive and getting it ready for print, Jihad (James), Saba, Dawood Bey, Raddic, Aaron (Fats), Tommie Knight and the whole Kpf family, Mr. Ronnie Dawson...and last but surely not the least, Brenda.

Prologue

The last words I remember hearing as an adolescent in my junior year of high school that seemed to change my social well-being, or so I thought were, "You will no longer attend Northeast High School young man!" As the words seemed to ooze from the principal's mouth, all I seemed to be able to muster up at that time was an ice cold look of resentment. No remorse, nor embarrassment, but 100% pure hatred for authority. I did feel a little bad for my father who was in attendance at this conference. He had a look on his face like he'd been betrayed by an ally to only find out that he was an enemy all along. I'll never forget that look.

That was the day after I'd been caught on school grounds in possession of marijuana. I was on my way to Burger King to get some breakfast at about 10:00am in the morning, because I was hungry, and it seemed like the day was going to be a bullshit day. Besides, my number one distributor didn't show today which meant I had to hand-to—hand the product my damn self, something I hated doing. Anyway, there I am at the corner of my school when truancy staff, teamed up with the local precinct police, blocked me in with their cars. My first instinct was to haul ass, but I figured I didn't do shit, so I thought. They proceeded to question me for identification and to look at the contents in my book bag. They really weren't asking me, because the short stubby officer, who seemed like he enjoyed this shit a little too much, already had my bag in his grasp. I was out-numbered, plus the shit in my bag wasn't in plain view, so if they did a once-over, I'd be cool. WRONG! This muthafucka ransacked my bag like he had a search warrant. Long story short, they found what they wanted. I didn't wanna cause a scene in front of the school, so I complied and let them cuff me, and off to the station I went. They hit me with a shitload of who's, what's and how's. I knew my rights. All they got from me was, "I would like to exercise my right to remain silent." "Suit yourself asshole," said Mr. Chubby Officer. So I was processed, finger-printed and put in a holding cell. Funny, all I could think about was my Burger King breakfast; instead, it was replaced by the 2nd District's finest hard-ass cheese sandwich with warm tea. "Damn this can't be happening… Let me hurry up and awake from this fucked up dream."

SORRY—NOT TODAY!

Chapter 1

Friday morning I'm walking around the house with my basketball shorts and Timberland boots on, enjoying these few days off from school. (Ding-Ding-Dong) I hear the doorbell ring so I turn the stereo down and see what's what. It's the mail man. I take the stack he hands me and start to flip through the mail. "... Bills... Bills... Bills... Bullshit... Bullshit... More Bills... More Bullshit... Department of Education- addressed to Mr. Russell Wade." "Hey, that's me" I said to myself. I ripped the envelope open to see what new school they had for a nigga. SHELLCROSS ALTERNATIVE LEARNING. Just what the hell I need, a school for the academically delinquent; the educationally challenged; or however you wanna sugar coat it. Bottom line, this school is for dumb muthafuckas or bad muthafuckas or both. Either way, that isn't me. I'm a bright nigga, who just happened to have a nice little hustle going on at one of the most prestigious schools in the Northeast District of Philadelphia; and now I'm headed to east Bumble Fuck to deal with these people. DAMN!

Sunday night I was having a little heart to heart discussion with my little brother Troy, who was three years younger than me, about life, decision making and how we gotta make wise choices because the wrong one could change your life forever. Only thing is I wasn't practicing any of the monkey shit I was feeding him. It just sounded like some big brother shit to say. I really did want good for my brother. He was in to shit like comics and Kung Fu, while my main interests were foreign hoes, foreign clothes and foreign cars. It's sort of ironic because I didn't grow up surrounded by that type of influence. My mother and father were hard workers who believed in discipline and providing their children with everything they needed and a little of what they wanted. We lived way better that a lot of my peers in my Germantown neighborhood. For starters, we owned our house, which was decked out with a modern kitchen and bathrooms. We had pretty good family contractors who remodeled everything in the house. So when you came to the Wade's residence, on the inside it looked like it belonged to a whole different neighborhood.

Hustling was never second nature to me. I don't know where I acquired the passion for it. We weren't allowed to hang out late and we always needed permission for just about anything. My father made a vow to himself not to let the streets take his family under. He work extra hard before that ever happened. So long hours as a manager at a local bank was well worth it to him. Deep down I always respected him for that. My mother was a fair-skinned pretty woman who worked for an insurance agency. So together they made a hell of a couple. I guess with a strong black woman in your corner it's nothing you feel like you can't accomplish. "…Ha Ha Ha-nigga you was running like Carl Lewis dog!" My brother Troy said, almost coming to tears with laughter. "Man fuck you", I shot back, "you would have done the same shit!" "Yeah, you right, better you than me Russ." We were discussing the events that took place after my mom, pop and my little bitch-ass brotha come to get me from the precinct.

"…Wade—you're being released", the guard over the loud speaker shouted. Man I felt like shit. I've been lying on this hard ass steel bench all day long and this funky-ass white dude gave me a serious migraine. This cat been in here all day for stealing two steak patties from Acme. He needed to be in a jungle not jail, as I thought to myself. (Cough-

cough-cough) "You be good young buck", said Mr. Funky White Man. "Alright dog, you be sick---I mean safe too."

"Damn, if it ain't one thing it's a mutha-fuckin notha", I said, referring to the Snoop Dogg song off his Doggy Style album. I made my way to the Plexiglas window where you retrieve all of your personal belongings you came in with. "Ok Mr. Wade, that's one belt, two pair of boot laces and $27.14. Just sign here", the guard said as he handed me a pen along with a plastic bag with all of my shit in it. "Straight through the double doors you'll find your family" he said with a smirk.

That's when I was hit with the bubble-guts. A very familiar feeling when you know your ass is about to be out. It felt like I had to shit, but I didn't eat anything all day, and that cheese sandwich was definitely not on my to-do list. I hated facing my family when I got into jams, especially my father.

See my mother could be persuaded, but good old pop dukes, you had nothing coming from him. He wasn't abusive or anything, but he spared no expense with yo ass when you decided to cut out of line. I had long grown out ass whooping's, but this was an exception. I'd never gotten arrested with drugs before, so I didn't know what to expect. I wasn't ruling out the possibility of an ass-kicking.

"Here goes nothing", I huffed. To my surprise behind door number 1, stood my Mom and brother, no Dad. "…He must be in the car," I thought to myself. All my mother said was "Are you alright? Do you have all of your belongings?" I kept my head down in shame and just nodded yes. Really I was contemplating my next move.

There was no way I was going to get beat down on an empty stomach.

As we exited the precinct I quickly scanned the vicinity. I noticed my pop about 20 feet away sitting in the car with a blank look on his face. Now I was bitching. I bent down to lace my boots... Think-Think-Think. My mind was racing. How can I get out of this? Once my shoes were tied tight I said, "Mom I forgot my book bag in there." She said, "I'll get it, go on over to the car." As soon as she headed for the steps I took off running. "Russell stop", she screamed. Not in a million years I thought. "You won't fuck me up tonight!" I managed to push out while darting in and out of traffic.

See here's my rationale to the whole situation: my Pop's is 201 pounds, about 5'11. Me, I'm 5'6 maybe 130 pounds, on a good day. The shit ain't mathematical. Plus the nigga got a mean right hand. I'll just give 'em time to cool off a bit. Makes sense right? RIGHT! I look over my shoulder while I'm running and look who it is, my silly ass brother. He's not really on my tail but close enough to see which direction I'm heading. I slow down and grab him by the shirt, "Look man this shit is serious, stop following me dog, go back to the car." My brother really cared about me, but now was not the time. Unless he planned on taking whatever punishment I had in store, then its best he let me tend to my escape route.

Once He backed off and I ran out of eye sight, I hustled myself across a busy intersection to a nearby pay phone, almost getting ran over by a Buick LaSabre. The sun had just went down and I was running around all suspicious. I got myself together and headed to the pay phone. "...SHIT" I only had .14 cents in change." I strolled

9

to a convenient store to break a dollar. I grabbed a .25 cent Hug and some hot chips and made my way back to the pay phone to call my Italian friend Vinny who I've known since elementary school. "He should be able to help me out", I said. (215)…- 3217, ring-ring. "Hello, is Vinny home?" I asked. "No he isn't can I take a message?" his mother responded. "Can you tell him Russ called please?", "Oh, hi Russ, I sure will", "Thanks, Bye." FUCK-FUCK-FUCK-FUCK! Where the hell is he, I fumed. He's probably at basketball practice. I kept it moving anyway heading towards his house. I figured by the time I got there he should be home.

Now I'm headed ten blocks towards my friend Vinny's crib. He's been the only white friend I've had in a while. Basically the only white friend I've had period. We go way back to elementary school where kids from the inner city were yellow bussed (cheese bus, as we liked to call them) to the schools in the more fortunate neighborhoods. It was called the Desegregation Program, which was supposed to allow inner city kids a change at receiving an education at some of the more privileged school districts. That was bullshit though. See the whole scheme was that schools have budgets and they also receive certain funds that comes in the form of grants to help pay for certain activities in the schools such as trips, books, computers, etc. The only problem is that you need students to fill the classrooms in order to be a benefactor of these grants. Well at this time all the white kids put together, only accounted for half the entire schools potential population. That's where we come in. They figured if they got minorities to come up we can still function like in our regular programs and look like humanitarians at the same time. We were basically being used.

10

My grandmother seen this whole plot way before it was in the makings. She tried to encourage my family, as well as others, not to bite into it. No one listened of course, and in the process our neighborhood schools suffered tremendously. Everyone was getting transferred to the "White Schools" so you know where the money went? You got it—WHITEY VILLE! Now this little project didn't of course stop the white teachers from having grudges about us being there. See racism never died. It just manipulated its way through other channels, so black students suffered. The teachers didn't understand us or where we came from, nor did we understand them for that matter. So while I achieved academically, I had behavior issues. Nevertheless, I made some good friends, Vinny being one.

We played ball mostly together, plus he enjoyed my mom's home cooking that she used to pack for me. He's an Italian kid and they say they have a little black in them anyway. They'll never admit it, but that's what it is. Anyway, his parents took a real liking to me. I was always polite and respectful. Vinny's dad used to play basketball with us. I used to bust his ass. Vinny and I did a lot together. We go back to sunflower seeds and lemon head candy. He used to look out for me on test day and let me cheat off of him. Me, being the good friend that I was, used to hold down some of the fly girls for him so he could sneak some feels in when we played "Catch-A-Girl-Freak-A-Girl." See Vinny was sort of a chubby kid and didn't particularly run very fast, so he was more than happy with my assistance. Those were good days. We've been cool ever since.

Ring-Ring-Ring-Ring… "Damn Vinny, where you at baby boy", I said into the pay phone receiver. I was at a phone booth around the corner from his house. He picked up on like the umpteenth ring. "…Hello, who is this?" Vinny answered exhausted. "…Yo man what up" I said. "Ain't nothing Russ, my moms told me you called my nigger." "What I tell your cracker ass about that nigger shit dog, you ain't black mafucka. Besides its nigga, not nigger. That's with an A not an E.R. Get it right before I slap ya face off," I said. "My bad, I ain't mean to offend you dog." "Aight, aight--enough apologizing. I'm in a fucked up situation." "What is it Russ, you got some girl pregnant or something?" "Nah man-in fact I'm around the corner from your house right now, meet me halfway."

He agreed and we both hung up. As he met me, I explained to him what had gone down stemming from the morning of my arrest. He told me he'd seen the cop cars, but didn't know who got pinched (Italian phrase for arrested). Luckily for me no one saw anything. I couldn't take being humiliated on top of being caught by truancy police. I asked him to let me chill at his place just for tonight. His peeps were cool so he assured me it wouldn't be a problem. Good, now I could triple S—shit, shower and sleep. Lord knows tomorrow will be a whole new episode.

After I showered and put some food in my belly we decided to play some video games. "Yo Vinny, what did you tell ya peoples about me needing to stay the night?" "I just told them you and your Dad had a big fight and you didn't want to stay home." "I appreciate it dog", I said before giving him a pound. "No problem my nigg—I mean my man." I looked at Vinny and just smiled. "Yo Vin, tomorrow right, I might be expelled if the police notify the school. If so I need you to pick up my money from everybody that owes me alright?" "Yeah aright Russ, business for you as usual huh?" "And you know this maaaannnnn," I said, like Smokey from the movie Friday. It was getting late so we decided to wrap the game up and get some sleep. Tomorrow it would be on and poppin'.

Time to face the music. "… Troy-Troy-Troy" my father yelled. I think he liked to hear himself yell. For whatever reason he did it, it worked at getting our attention. "Troy don't make me call you again, you know what time it is, you got school tomorrow." "Huh?" my brother said. "Boy if you can huh, you can hear. Get ya narrow ass up here and in this bed." I almost forgot it was that late. "Go on ahead dog-before Dad has a heart attack," I said. "Aight I'm out, let me know how ya new school is," my brother said. "Aight man I will" I told him. He went to his room upstairs and I crept in my room which was located in the basement. My Dad reconstructed it like 8 years earlier, just to give me some privacy and some sort of independence. It was half the length of the entire basement and was decked out with wall to wall carpet, matching Du Pont painted walls, a full length couch and floor to ceiling closets. My room was hooked up.

I had all my favorite heroes posted on my walls; Allen Iverson and Bruce Lee. And you know a teenager's room wouldn't be complete without the infamous Lil' Kim poster. You know the one where her coochie looks like a fist balled up in leopard print panties. I loved my room. So I hope my pops ain't get no bright ideas about taking that away from me as punishment since he let me slide by without whooping my ass. I took off my boots and pants and laid across my Queen Size bed looking up at my drop ceiling. "…Wheew—Shell Cross—Here I come."

Chapter 2

I awoke to the annoying sound of my alarm clock. I guess that's what they're designed to sound like. My pop yelled at the top of the stairs for me to be ready if I wanted a ride to the bus stop. I didn't argue 'cause I didn't feel like catching the bus to get on another one. Plus he had a white Maxima with a bangin' system, so I really didn't mind pulling up on everybody with that. There were two designated pick up stops where a yellow bus would provide us with rides to the Franklin Mills section of Philadelphia, which ain't no hop, skip and a jump. One of the stops was Frankford Bus Terminal, and Wyoming Ave & Broad St., the one where I was headed.

I didn't have to be there until 9:00am and let out time was 1:30pm at Shell Cross. "…This school must be bullshit" I said as I brushed my wavy hair. I figured any school asking you to be there that late and letting you out that early had to be a joke, but who was I to complain. I just wanted to attain whatever credits I needed to get out of there and back to a regular school. 7:30am my Dad was honking his horn for me to come on. I grabbed some money out of my dresser drawer and snatched my book bag and Walkman. On the way out the door I grabbed me a pack of Pop Tarts and jumped in the front seat of the car.

It was a quiet ride to the bus stop. I was deep in thought while a bit of anxiety began to seep in. I just wanted to regain my father's trust by doing well at this school. That's what I planned to do. We pulled up at the corner of Broad St & Wyoming Ave., right where the Dunkin Donuts was. My Dad told me to have a good day and then bounced to work. There I am—me against the world. At least I was dressed nice. You won't catch me at a new school looking like Steve Erkel or some shit. I had an all-white Polo rugby pullover with 3 buttons, some crispy pencil pocket Guess jeans, and some fresh butter scotch Timbs on. My book bag was even Timberland, so my confidence was up on my appearance.

The scene at the bus stop looked like a club let out. Niggaz were everywhere—a few girls sprinkled through the crowd. I noticed this chick with an extremely phat ass standing outside the Dunkin Donuts. I wanted to crack on her, but I decided not to. I was kind of out of my element. I wasn't used to big crowds. I hoped she was going to the same school I was. Her ass was so phat it looked like if the cops were coming, you could hide your pistol under her ass cheeks. DAMN!

We both stared at each other as I walked in the store to get a breakfast sandwich. When I came out, the yellow bus was boarding its passengers. So I diverted my attention to the bus. Half the crowd that was standing out there dispersed, which was good, I hated crowded buses anyway. One thing I noticed while getting on the bus was that they didn't take names. I figured who in their right mind would just volunteer to go to this school unless they had to. So I get on and I go straight to the back of the bus to sit down, when I hear this voice… "Nobody better sit in my seat", some big nigga said. I had no idea which seat was his so I just sat in the second to the last seat, and put my headphones on, but didn't turn my music on yet. I wanted to be on point around all these unfamiliar mafuckas.

Next thing I did was size every dude up that got on the bus. This is something I did to determine who I thought would be a potential problem, if it ever came down to it. No real threats though, a few big niggas, but I could handle it.

My philosophy was this—we all claim to be men, so in order to gain respect we sometimes gotta put fear aside to do what we gotta do, as men. I intended to do as such. Anyhow, fuck how big a nigga is, ain't too many muscles in his chin, so if you jam one home on it hard enough, more times than not, he'll bite the dirt. As long as you know you can take an ass whuppin' at any time that should keep you grounded. I really wasn't worried about that though, I was a likeable dude, plus my 'bout game wasn't too shabby either. All of a sudden something or should I say someone broke my chain of thought. "…Excuse me, is this seat taken?" It was the girl with the really phat ass. Being the new guy does have its benefits, I thought. "… I don't think it is" was my only response. She caught me off guard 'cause usually I'd have some super fly shit to say in return.

I got a chance to really see her close up. She wasn't winning any beauty contests but she was far from a mud duck. Whatever her face lacked, her body definitely made up for. I mean for a high school girl this chick had a body like a grown ass woman. She definitely could've been in "Big Pimpin" video with no rap. For real!

"Hi my name is Tasha. What school you coming from?" My mind went racing again. Why is it that every part of the city gotta aggressive girl named Tasha in it with a super phat ass? "Huh" was my only response. I thought to myself, 'why does this girl have me speechless.' "What school are you coming from?" she said. I answered, "Oh I'm from Northeast and you", she replied "Ben Franklin." "Oh yeah, my man Gary goes there." Suddenly we were interrupted. "Yo Tash, what up wit a girlfriend for me—huh?" "I told you Jules, I got you boy," Tasha said annoyed. She was now talking to the boy behind us who

16

said nobody better sit in his seat. This nigga looked like a grown ass man. I wanted to say, damn what you been here since the school opened dog? I kept it to myself though. Dude was big as shit too; I see why niggaz let him have his own seat. Tasha whispered to me that Jules (real name Julius) was her friend, sort of like her big brother. "This is my friend Julius—Julius this is…" Tasha whispered, "I didn't get your name" I whispered back, "That's cuz I never gave it to you." She smiled at my sarcasm. "What up, my name is Russ," I said as Jules and I shook hands. "What up Russ" he said; and that was that. "Anyway Jules, I'll get Tiffany to call you tonight" Tasha said, "bet", said Jules.

Interrupted again. "Yo Russ—what up dog it's me Kenny." Who the fuck is Kenny, I thought to myself. "You don't remember me from Northeast?" "Oh yeah, what up" I said. I lied; I didn't know this cornball ass nigga from a hole in the wall. "Can I see your Walkman," Kenny said. "Naw my batteries are dead homey." Another lie, but fuck it. If it's nothing I hate more, it's a joe familiar, dick-riding ass nigga whose only speaking to you cuz he want something. Beat it kid is what I really wanted to say. Then I started singing… "I hate a Joe-Joe nigga, no dough nigga", then Tasha finished by saying, "Whip say Six, but really a four nigga." We both started laughing quietly, as we sang the rap song by Philly native Beanie Siegle. I felt like I knew Tasha for longer than I did. She had this personality that made you wanna be around her—not to mention that bubble of hers. She's the type of chick you could kick it with all day and then fuck all night. At least that's what I was hoping for.

We talked for the next half hour until I grew a little tired from the long ass ride. The school was like an hour and some change away. I put my head on the window and gazed out onto the city streets. I guess Tasha was tired too because, out of nowhere, she laid her head across my lap. I was taken aback by her gesture, but I played it cool. I just put my hand on her shoulder and kept staring out the window like it was nothing. The whole time I'm excited as hell. I know for a fact she had to feel my dick get hard and push against her ear. Obviously, she didn't seem to take offense by it because in no time she was asleep. I took that as time to observe my surroundings. I saw a few haters staring my way with the 'ice grill', but they only got one right back. What did I care; I had the baddest chick on the bus's head in my lap. Not bad for day one, huh.

I looked back to see if big ass Julius was trippin'. He just put his hands up and shrugged his shoulders, as if to say 'what do you want me to do." So I smiled and shrugged my shoulders right back. I turned back around and dozed off myself; so much for being on point. We finally arrived at Shell Cross. "Wake up sleepy head", I heard Tasha say while poking me in my stomach. I was really up, but I kept my eyes closed so she could keep touching me. "Russss wake up boo." Damn I liked the way she called my name. I finally opened my eyes when I put my mouth right near her ear and whispered, "Somebody gotta be last, and it might as well be us." Then I kissed her earlobe and then sat back to bask in my pimp glory, while a big smile crossed my lips. 'That's the Russ I know' I whispered to myself. We were the last to exit the bus. "Ladies first ma" as she walked in front of me I admired her ass again. Looked like two volleyballs stuffed in a pair of Sergio Valente jeans. I said a small prayer to myself, 'please God make all the girls at Shell Cross like Tash.'

18

Chapter 3

When we all exited the bus we were ordered to proceed to the lunch room for a standard weapons check/search. I thought, this shit seems like jail more than school. Tasha went her way to be searched with the girls while the boys went their way. While waiting my turn I noticed a couple of dudes sitting on the ground with handcuffs on. They must've been the unlucky ones who got caught. This shit reminded me of East Side High from the movie 'Lean on Me." Kids running around the lunchroom cursing, slap boxing, and ice grillin'—all while a search was being conducted a few feet away.

After I was cleared I found me an empty spot at a table. I briefly looked around before sitting on top of the table. After everybody was cleared from the search, a staff member along with some cafeteria workers helped pass out juices and donuts to everyone for breakfast. It was 9:30am and we had 15 minutes to eat before beginning with our first period class. 9:45 came in a flash and everybody went their way, except me.

It was the middle of the year (March) and I didn't have a roster. I tapped one of the staff members on the shoulder to get his attention so maybe he could direct me somewhere to get a roster. This scary ass guy jumped like I had a knife or something. I quickly put my hands up and said. "Hold on buddy, I'm just wondering where I can find the main office because I don't have a roster. I'm new here." The guy kindly said, "Sorry about that kid. Walk through those doors, it's the third door on your left." "Thanks Mister." As I made my way to the office I noticed that the building I was in was extremely clean and quiet. I later found out that the school was divided into two sections. One for the students who wanted to learn and go on to a normal life; and the other section was for the kids who didn't give a shit about anything. I knew what section I was staying in.

At the front desk of the main office I explained to the receptionist that I didn't have a roster and that today was my first day. The lady asked for my full name and birth date. Within a few minutes I had my official roster. First period—Math/Social Studies (Room 212). As I diddy-bopped down to room 212, I peeked in a few other classrooms, which held about 12 to 15 students. Rather small I thought, but I guess that's the way they want it. This way the teacher doesn't get bombarded with troubled kids and in turn the kids get the necessary attention to pass. Good system. I approached room 212 and knocked on the door. A middle-aged white woman opened it and introduced herself.

"Hi, my name is Mrs. Anastasia, but everyone calls me Mrs. A." She stepped in the hallway for a minute to explain a few things before introducing me to the rest of the class. "You must be Russell Wade?" "Yep you must be right," I said playfully. She seemed like a nice woman, a little hyper, but nice. "Well Mr. Wade this will be your homeroom. We have three one hour classes, which will consist of a math, history, and physical education, most of the people here will be in your classes. Lunch is at 11:30, for one hour. Now that that has been said, do you have any questions before meeting your home room?" "Nope," I said quickly. "Well then, here we go… Class I would like to introduce you to our new student Russell Wade. Please introduce yourself class." Everyone got up to introduce themselves.

For this to be an alternative school, it sure was a nice bit of girls there. I couldn't remember not one dudes name. My focus was on the chicks, and they seemed to be feeling me too. Whoever said light-skin niggaz were played out was a fucking hater. None of these girls really looked all that good, but I loved the attention from their eye contact. I took the only seat available, which happened to be right in front of the teacher. It really didn't matter though. The class was too small for any sneaky shit to go down unnoticed, besides I didn't come to play games.

Mrs. A. passed out the work assignments to all the students. I looked down at the work sheet and said to myself, "damn this shit is super easy." I finished the worksheet in like 20 minutes. The remaining class took the whole period. 'I guess these kids really need to be here', I thought. Me, I knew I didn't belong. I just had to blend in until it was my time to raise the fuck up outta here. Mrs. A. handed me another worksheet, which I finished ever faster than the first one.

At 10:30 the bell rang for our second period class. I stayed behind to talk to Mrs. A. about a few things involving my stay. Like how long do I have to stay at Shell Cross, and how can I speed up the process for getting out. She explained that the curriculum is based on a point and color card system. Each color card represents a total of points accomeulated by work assignments completed. There are three color cards: red, green and gold. For every 300 points you move up a card. Everyone starts out on red and ends with gold. Once you're at gold your application is submitted to the school board for recommendation of release to a regular provincial school. Once they make their decision, you can roll to whatever school that accepts your application. Easily put, the more work you do, the faster you get out. "That's all I needed to hear Mrs. A." I jetted to my second period class.

Chapter 4

Things around the house were starting to look better as time went on. The tension between my father and I started to loosen up as well. Well, not completely. I overheard my mother and him discussing my behavior as of late. Pops described it as my rebellious stage while coming to manhood. From the sounds of it through the door, she agreed. He also assured her that these little stunts I've been pulling would no longer be tolerated. He didn't raise no drug dealers and if I couldn't live by his rules then he would kick me out…

Blah-Blah-Blah. It sounded like some shit from the Cosby Show when Theo got caught with a joint in his textbook. I was fully aware of what he was trying to get across to my Mom, 'stop defending that boy!' I eased my way back down the stairs and went to my room to think. See this ain't the first time I've been caught selling weed. It's just the only time I've been busted by the cops.

Ya see I've been selling weed since I was 14 in the 9th grade. I used to believe the things my father used to tell me about working an honest job to get what I wanted. He said it built integrity and showed responsibility and patience. For the most part I believed him. So I got a job. Actually two jobs. Nothing major, I worked at a clothing store and as a telemarketer. They paid pretty well, but they were time consuming. I didn't have time for anything else. So I decided to ditch one job and pick up a trade. Selling weed.

That shit wasn't that complicated either, see drugs really sell themselves. If I don't serve them, someone will. I'd rather it be me. So when I first got to Northeast my man from my hood introduced me to his man who was in his last year there. His name was T., from North Philly, and he had the school on smash with the weed. We became good friends as he schooled me to the game. I paid close attention at all times. I was intrigued. I even noticed some flaws in his operation, but kept it to myself.

See T. hand dealt everything, which I thought was risky, since his name had been poppin' for at least 3 years. Nevertheless, he was prepping me for a reason. He wanted me to take over. I was about to be the muthafuckin man. T. introduced me to a few of his clientele and would sell me quarter pounds to bag up and knock off. Things were going real good. I was making money, not as much as expected, but hey, you gotta crawl before you walk. Besides, next year would be my year anyway. And indeed it was.

The following year business was good. I was now coppin' pounds off T. and he would front me a half pound. Things were lovely, I had the market cornered. I had plenty of horses (distributors) working with my efforts. First I had two white boys, one skateboard freak and one regular nerd. They dealt with two different groups, but shared the same interest. They smoke weed. I needed every crowd in my pockets. Plus my man who was on the football team was down. He took care of that, plus the high school groupies who loved to smoke too. Then there was the loser crowd who did nothing but smoke all day. I had my man L. take care of them since he always came to school late and hung out in front of a convenient store all day.

There you have it. Northeast was officially on lock. If you smoked at school, 9 times outta 10, it came from yours truly. I handled all weight sells. It didn't matter to me if I sold anybody weight, because they couldn't move it anyway. My horses had it locked down. I even had a little white girl who smoked, that worked in the Principal's office. I used to hit her off with quarter ounces here and there. She basically was my ears in that office. I didn't want her selling shit. She is what you call a necessary expense. It was worth it. She put me down with raids and people droppin' info off at the Principal's office.

I was on my way home from school late on a Friday, as I do every Friday because business is extremely well on that day. Nobody seems to go home early. As I approach my house my Dad is standing on the porch like he waiting on me. He couldn't be mad; I always came home around 7:00pm on Fridays. Anyway, he said he needed to talk to me about a few things. He was totally calm, which brought my antennas up. When I walked to the dining room table I see my Mom crying. "What's going on here?" I asked. "This is," my father said, as he held up a plastic bag containing a pressed pound and a half of Arizona weed. I felt like the life had been sucked out of me. I'd been caught. "Empty your pockets boy", my Dad demanded. "Huh" I said. Before I knew it he reached in my pockets pulling out $2700 in small bills. I couldn't believe it. I'd been robbed for the first time. By my Moms and Pops. "That explains all this shopping you've been doing" my Dad said sarcastically. "Go to your room" he yelled.

As I jetted down stairs I heard my little brother in my room. "What the hell, you want to rob me too?" I said sarcastically. "Russ, I ain't do nuthin', but Mommy and Daddy said they found something." "Yeah I know" I replied. My room had been ransacked. Like a tornado hit it. Lamps knocked over, couch cushions over turned, clothes scattered everywhere, just a mess. I decided to take a deep breath and evaluate my losses. I told my brother to get out and let me think for a minute. "Why I gotta go Russ", Troy pleaded. "Look man, just get out and I'll buy you a pair of sneakers tomorrow" I told him. "Okay, you promise man?" I told him "Bye, before I change my mind!" "Aight Russ, aight' Troy said. Once he left I checked to make sure wasn't anything else missing. I first checked my drop ceiling where I had 6 pounds of Arizona and a half pound of kine-bud stacked up there. 'Good, they ain't find that', I said with relief. Then I checked the inside of my queen size mattress to see if my stash was still intact. 'Perfect' $9800 in crispy hundred dollar bills with money wraps on each $1000. I then looked in the mirror and said to myself, 'Stop bitching nigga, it could be worse!'

After getting that out the way, I went in my closet to start hanging some of my clothes back up. That's when I noticed that all my sneakers were gone…every pair. Just then my Dad opened the door, "All them sneaks you bought with that drug money, I threw them away, and by the way, I called your job and told them you won't be returning. Seems you don't know what real values and responsibilities are. From now on I want ya ass home right after school. If not you got problems." And just like that he left. I felt a tear run down my left cheek. It wasn't about what was missing but rather the fact that I was being played like shit and couldn't do anything about it. I was beyond furious. From that minute I made myself a promise to turn my hustle game up one thousand!

Chapter 5

Shell Cross wasn't half as bad as I thought it would be. In fact I kind of liked it. We had a good basketball team and even had a swimming pool. This school was lovely. And they had chicks that I was quite friendly with. The guys there seemed like they had no ambition to do anything, but stay dumb and stay at Shell Cross. Even though the school was cool, it was no place for Russell Wade.

Now the girls, they were different. Once you got to know them, they were extremely intelligent, just happened to be violent. They loved me because I always kept it real with them and listen to what they had to say, like I gave a damn. One Spanish mami said I was the only man in her life that paid that much attention to her. She wanted to be my girl, but I couldn't do it. Free lancing had better benefits. Plus it wouldn't be fair to Tasha. She liked me too.

I completed a month at Shell Cross and I was already working on my green card. I would be leaving sooner than I thought, I said to myself. As the bell sounded to end the day, I made plans to stop by Northeast to check up on my business. I had to set up something with Vinny to keep everybody supplied while I was gone. Time to collect. When I got off the bus at Northeast, I saw L. on his post, which made me proud. The news I got from him was disturbing though. Things turned disastrous.

Niggaz got greedy and started moving against each other like they all didn't work for me. Without my presence, things just fell apart. No one bothered to take care of the girl in the Principal's office, therefore she supplied no more info, which caused a lot of problems. A few people got arrested, people got expelled and my pockets suffered. To top it off L. was short. He smoked more than he sold. Once I rounded up what was left of my workers, I collected all they had, plus whatever product too. I explained to them that this could no longer continue. From now on they had to buy everything, if not, oh well. I was taking losses like crazy. Not anymore! Everybody had my number. I told them good luck and to hit me if needed. Then I left pissed. Everything I worked for was over.

On my way home I stopped by my stash house, which really was just an abandoned house that I put a pad lock on the door and started keeping my shit there. My old head Samir told me to never shit where you eat, so that's why I got it in the first place. I also figured why keep money at my home. If anything were to happen to the stash there, I would be finished.

Since me and Tasha were kicking it real tough, I got her a little $500/month apartment and stashed money there too. She wouldn't know about the money being there anyway. Plus I could fuck that phat ass whenever I wanted. Her parents never gave a damn whether she came or went anyway. When she moved in, it was all good. Besides now I had a place to chill sometimes when Pops started buggin'. I still kept a few grand with me at my parents crib. I had to have something with me at all times; only money, no drugs. I couldn't afford getting caught up again.

On my way to my peoples crib I got a page from Tasha. When I got in the house I threw my book bag on the couch and called her. She wanted me to come over and make love to her. I hated when she said 'make love', because it made it seem as if we were a couple, when we were just cool. She was free to do her and so was I. As long as she didn't have no niggaz in the crib, I was cool. I decided to let the comment slide and told her I'd be over. Since my parents wouldn't be home for another 4 hours I had time. I was getting tired of all this sneaking around and shit. I was making more money than both my folks together and I gotta creep to get some pussy. The shit didn't make sense to me. But still I wasn't ready to be put out. I didn't even have a car yet. I made that my next thing to do.

Tasha's apartment was located in the upscale neighborhood of Mt. Airy, right near Lincoln Drive, which was cool 'cause I needed the privacy. When I got to the door, I put my key in and went straight to the refrigerator. At the bottom was a little compartment on the outside where I kept my stash. It was 3ft by 6in; which was more than enough room. I had $27,000 already tucked away. I put the $4000 I got today in with it. $31,000 at 16 years old-not bad. Plus I had $5,300 at my Mom's crib and whatever weed I had in the abandoned house. I heard Tasha in the other room, so I finished and put everything back in order and joined her in the bedroom.

"Did you miss me baby?" she said. "Damn I seen you at school all day girl" I said dryly. She sucked her teeth. 'Sike girl I was just bullshittin and you know this maaann" I said like Chris Tucker. "Boy you play too much!" "Girl you know I can't get enough of you." She said "Russ do you love me?" I answered, "Of course I do, why?" "No Russ, do you really love me?" she insisted. I thought about it for a minute. Maybe it was the fact that I was possibly leaving Shell Cross in a few months or maybe the fact that I treated her better than any man had. Whatever it was, she seemed serious. "Of course I do

Tasha." Just then a beautiful smile crossed her face. Tasha
was actually beautiful; she just wore too much makeup at
times. Today I got her all natural and she was much prettier
that way. I guess I did love her though. Maybe not the way
she loved me, but I did have love for the girl. I just don't
think I was in love with her.

Tasha was laying there in some French-cut lace
panties with a black wife beater on. I laid her on the bed
and ripped her panties off in one motion. I was feeling real
horny for some reason. I lifted her tank top over her head,
so she was completely nude. I began sucking on her nice C-
cup breasts while nibbling on her nipples. Her light brown
skin reminded me of Claudette Ortiz from City High and
her ass was like J-Lo times 2. My dick was hard like
concrete, as she was rubbing it through my jeans. I stood up
and stripped butt naked and went right back to sucking her
titties. She was moaning softly while rubbing my hair. I
licked all the way down her stomach until I got to her
shaven pussy, which was drippin' wet at this point. I gently
started licking her clit as I inserted two fingers in her pussy.
I took my fingers out and sucked her sweet juices off. She
started gyrating her hips towards my face, so I applied
more pressure on her clit with my tongue. "Oooh baby,
make mommy come for you….Oooh I wanna come on your
face." I was oblivious to anything she said. I had a mission.
I sucked her pussy until she came all over my face and
tongue. I then flipped her over and ate her ass and pussy
from the back. She had two more orgasms before she
begged for me to put this heavy dick in her.

I pulled the back of her hair and slowly squeezed
my dick in her tight walls. I felt pussy muscles clamp on
my dick. I almost exploded, but held firm. I fucked her

30

slow, until she begged me to fuck her harder. "…Fuck me harder daddy-I've been so bad daddy… Please fuck me hard daddy!" I couldn't argue with the woman, as I picked up the pace. Her ass was so phat I almost slipped out a few times. I stayed in that position for about 20 minutes. "… Tash-I'm comeming ma!" She just threw her ass cheeks smack down on my dick until I filled her up with the biggest nut I've ever busted. Every drop went in her. For some reason, I believe she did that intentionally.

Chapter 6

Once my Dad left out my room and I made a vow to step my grind up, I finished cleaning up. I still had clothes and sneakers over at my man Kacy's house across the street. At that point I didn't want them anymore. I was angry and motivated. I had a point to prove to my Pop, as well as myself. One monkey doesn't stop any show! I called Kacy's house to let him know that he could keep whatever I had left over there.

"Hello, can I speak to Kacy?"

"This is him"

"What up nigga, it's Russ"

"What up Russ?"

"Nothing. You can keep whatever clothes I got at ya crib."

"Why what's going on man? You aight?"

I banged on him. I had to get my plan in order. First things first, let me add up all my losses. I owe T. $600 for the weed my peoples took. Another $2700 in money they took, plus $800 for the weed, and $900 in sneakers. Total... $5000, plus I'm out of a job. After that I called up all my horses and told them to all meet me in front of the school an hour early. I had planned something.

After I got off the phone I walked around the corner to my barber shop. I needed some advice. My barber, Samir, was a cool Muslim brother who had been in the game for a while before taking his religion seriously and calming down. I told him my situation while he gave me a two with the grain. "Young buck you can't shit where you eat at Ahkee. If you're gonna be staying at home you can't keep hiding thousands of dollars worth of stuff there without causing suspicion." "What should I do then," I asked. "You need to find a stash house" he replied. That's sounded like a good idea. I didn't know why I didn't come up with it earlier. Once Samir finished my hair, I paid him and headed to the door. "Be safe Russ" he told me. "I'll try" I said, and rolled out.

I knew of the ideal stash house. There was an abandoned home around the corner from my house. I went around to take a look at it. It was perfect. There was a pad lock on the door, so I took a crowbar to it and knocked it off. Ten minutes later I came back with a lock and key of my own. The good thing was that the lock was on the back door, so this way no one would see me coming or going. It was on.

Later that night I snuck out of my house with two bags in hand with 6 pounds of weed and close to $10,000 in cash in them, heading to my new stash house. It was 3 floors high and had been vacant since I could remember. I put everything on the 3rd floor. I sat there with 3 candles and a million little jars. My plan was to put everything in jars now. Nobody was selling them, and this way it gave the illusion you were getting more. Everything was going 3 for $10 anyway. It was just a matter of time before I became hood rich. "…See Dad—see what you done started" I said aloud. I looked at my watch, 3:15am… four hours until show time.

Chapter 7

I woke up groggy at 6:15am. I only got 40 minutes of sleep last night. I knew I had to get up though. Business first! I got up and brushed my teeth and threw on a structure hoody with some Guess jeans, grabbed my book bag and was headed out of the house at 6:30, on my way to my stash house. I hoped everyone was on time.

When I arrived at the school, everyone was all waiting on me. Good! I explained to everyone the plan and what was expected. Also I threw in a 10% raise for everyone if things went according to plan. "Okay everybody, let's get this money" I said. The next two weeks were like the first down south. I went through 40 pounds of gank in less than 20 days. My plan was working wonders. Everybody was making loot. Things were beautiful. Even kids from other schools were coming to cop. My prices couldn't be beat.

It got so crazy, people were outside my classroom window trying to get my attention so they could buy. I could barely concentrate on my school work. My grades dropped from B's to C's. I was really slipping. Plus Northeast teachers had a real habit of contacting parents when their student's grades dropped. I had already taken care of that. I gave a list of phone numbers to my little buddy in the Principal's office and told her to switch those with the ones my parents had given them in the beginning of the school year. All calls went either to my cell phone voice mail or my pager. I was on point.

February was my best month, right after mid-terms. Everybody was sort of relieved that they were finally done and over with, plus there was a winter class trip for the seniors coming up, not to mention our football team won the championship. Much need for celebration! I bullshit you not, I sold 58 pounds of weed in one month. Things were definitely good. Northeast was a fuckin' gold mine and I was the Master Mind behind it. No one ever had it poppin' like I did in such a short time. This was only my 3rd year there.

March 1st, everyone was back from the senior trip and things were back to normal. My pockets were extremely fat! I had about $82,000 stashed all over my little hideout. I was a pretty good saver, mainly because my super suspicious Pop was all in my ass. I wasn't mad though, I liked looking at my money pile up. Besides I was the only kid at school with a Sub-Marina Rolex with a 4-carat diamond bezel worth $12,500. The diamonds were so clear people thought it was fake. I hated walking around with $12,500 watch and no car. That would soon change.

As soon as I was walking out of my 3rd period class, I noticed this white girl named Trish headed my way. She told me all about the senior trip she went on and how much fun she had and wished I could've joined her. Trish was a white girl with a black girl body. I should've fucked her, but never got around to it. Anyway she was flirting like crazy, with this little ass skirt on. So I decided to give her what I felt she wanted. Once everyone was in their 4th period class, I told her to meet me in the boy's room. She happily led the way.

While she was walking in front of me I slipped my hand up her skirt to touch her pussy. All she did was poke her butt up while I did it. She pushed the boy's door open. Empty! She immediately got on her knees in one of the stalls and unzipped my pants. I pulled out and shoved my dick right in her mouth. She gave me her best porno face and said "Mmmm, you taste good Russ baby." Trish was a real pro. She licked my balls and everything. She took my dick out her mouth and jerked it, while slapping herself in the face with it. I was loving it! "… I want you to come in my mouth," she said. Three seconds later she got her wish.

As I was pulling up my pants Trish grabbed them and said, "Baby I want you to fuck me." "Not now Trish, I got somewhere to be." "Please, you can put it anywhere you like," she begged. That certainty got my attention. I looked at my Roley and I had 10 minutes before I had to meet T. out front. "Alright girl you got it," I said. I bent Trish over the toilet and told her to open her ass cheeks. She did what she was told and said, " Oooh baby fuck me in my pretty ass!" That's what I did. I went dead in her ass for like 5 good minutes. I shot my load in her ass, whipped my dick and kissed her on the forehead. Then I bolted out of there to meet T. in front of the school. We had some official business to tend to.

Chapter 8

I kissed Tasha on her lips and headed for the door. I pulled out a couple hundred bucks and told her I'd call her once I got home. She told me she loved me again before I bounced. When I set foot in my house I called Tash to let her know I got in, and then I told her I'd call back a little later on. "Russ" my Dad was yelling for me at the top of the steps. "Yeah, here I come." What the hell was he yelling for? He started off by telling me how he didn't think I changed and that he found my Rolex in my dresser drawer. "If you can't abide by the rules of this house, I think you better leave" he said. Damn, this guy stays snooping around.

"Dad, I didn't even do anything. That watch ain't even real," I said. He knew better and just stared at me like I was insulting his intelligence. I took this as an opportunity to show my independence, so I quietly packed my shit and headed back to Tasha's. No one stopped me from leaving either. I called Tasha and told her I'd be coming by and I'd explain everything once I got there. Tasha met me in the lobby of the complex to help me with my bags.

"Baby what happened?" she asked curiously. "My Pops started tripping and told me I had to roll." She said, "I'm sorry to hear that boo." I knew she was fronting. She was happy as hell I was moving in. She'd mentioned it one too many times before. "Yeah, it's cool though, I'll be aight" I said coldly. When we got inside the apartment, I threw my bags on the floor. I still had a few bags at my parent's house that I didn't bring. I planned on getting those tomorrow.

I made my way to the bedroom and laid across it. After I laid there for a minute, I kicked my boots off, got up and headed to the shower to wash up. I still had sex on me from earlier when I fucked Tasha all crazy. She was in the kitchen trying to fix something to eat. Tasha wasn't much of a cook, but she tried. Truth is, couldn't no one cook better than my Mom.

When I came out of the shower I was drying my hair, when I took notice of the pancakes, turkey sausage, eggs and orange juice all laid out nice and neat on the kitchen table. I was in the mood for a little breakfast anyway. Once I dried off and got dressed, I headed for the kitchen where Tasha was waiting for me. I had on a dab of my favorite cologne; Vera Wang for men. Tash loved the way it smelled on me too. "You smell good baby" she commented. "I know" as I smiled back. We both sat and ate for about 30 minutes, while talking about everything from sports to where our relationship was heading. We finished off the night by watching Rocky 4. I just held her in my arms in the bed; it felt good being there with her. We went to bed rather early. We both had school in the morning.

"Tash, get up," I said while brushing my teeth. "Alright, alright, alright, I'm up," she said. As we got ready for school I had checked my voice mail because I was waiting to hear from T. "You have no new messages" the operator for my mail service said. Click-Click-Click, as I locked up the apartment door. We headed to the bus stop. As we got off the bus at Broad & Wyoming, it looked like the scene from my first day. It was approaching June and the weather was nice this morning. Tasha and I walked side by side to the Dunkin Donuts to grab some orange juices. We saw Julius on our way. So I told her to go ahead and get our drinks while I talked to Jules. "What up Jules?" I said. For some reason he had been acting sort of strange towards me lately. I knew it couldn't be because of Tasha, he said they were like brother and sister. Besides I never really told him any of our business anyway. Unless, Tasha told him something. "What up Russ" as he shook my hand and gave me a phony smile. Something was definitely up with him; I paid it no mind though. Tasha came out with our drinks as the bus pulled up. Tasha walked right past Julius without speaking. Something was really fishy. I decided to hold my tongue about it.

As soon as I got to my seat with Tasha, I put my headphones on and laid across her lap and chilled out with some R&B shit. While riding, I noticed Tasha kept turning around toward the back row. I guess she was saying something to Jules. What I didn't know. I really didn't care at that point. I had way too many other issues to worry about this funny game they were playing. I took my ass to sleep for almost an hour.

Chapter 9

"Glaciers of Ice... Glaciers...Of... Ice..." by Ghostface was pumping out of the system of T.'s car as I got in. "This is my shit dog," I said while rapping along to the CD. I asked, 'so T., what's poppin' dog? What was the emergency page for?"

"I got good news playboy. My Mexican connect just hit me and told me he had 500 pounds of that shit for us for $100,000, that's $200 a pound dog."

"Straight up T. you for real?"

"Dog, I ain't bullshitting. I've been trying to put this shit together for months now."

"How much you need from me T.?"

"I was hoping we could go half, I don't really trust anybody else like that or who would trust me like that besides you? This could be our big move!"

"50 grand—God Damn! I only got 48 grand in the tuck, plus this 2 grand I got on me. That's my whole fucking stash."

"Hey man life is a gamble, you either in or you out?"

"You know I'm in baby, just please don't fuck this up!"

"You worry too much; I gotta get ready to take this money to Mexico by the day after tomorrow, so I'll be catching a flight tomorrow afternoon."

"Cool, I'll page you as soon as I get home from school."

"Aight Russ, hit me baby." I gave him a pound and exited his car. Beep-Beep-Beep... T. rolled down his window and said," I'll be by tomorrow morning to scoop you from your crib." "Aight" I said.

I was about to run into some serious paper if T. made good on this deal. Part of me felt as if I was making a big mistake. Part of me was feeling weird because that was the first time that I'd lied to T. by telling him I only had $50 grand to my name. I had damn near a buck by now, but he need not know all that. Biggie said it best, "Never let no one know how much doe you hold, cuz you know the chedda breed jealousy, especially if that man fucked up, get yo ass stuck up!"

My mind was no longer on school work after that conversation, so I decided to hang out in the lunch room for the remainder of the day. I sat at a table at the far end of the lunchroom with my head down eating a bag of Doritos's, sipping on a Hawaiian Punch, trying to be as inconspicuous as possible. I was observing everyone in the room and it seemed to me that no one really had any real ambition. Everyone was content at being mediocre. For me, being complacent wasn't an option. I had dreams and big plans. BIG FUCKING PLANS!

After school ended, I headed straight home. Up the block from my house was a Rite Aid which sold school supplies. I had to get a lunch box. "$8.95 please" the female cashier said. This lady had to be at least 15 years older than me, but she looked good. Toni Braxton good! "Would you like anything else sir?" she said.

41

"Yeah, your phone number," I said, as I handed her a $10 bill.

"You are too young for me young man."

"Says who?" I shot back.

"Says me, plus I'm married."

"You can't be happy, cuz you ain't wearing a ring." She looked embarrassed, so I left it alone. "I'll see you around gorgeous." Then I grabbed my lunch box and headed out the door without getting my change. From the look on her face, I must have been right. I was walking back towards my house when my beeper went off. It was my man L. I called him right back from a pay phone cuz my battery was dead on my cell.

"Yo L. what up?"

"What up Russ, I'm out I need something for tomorrow."

'Aight, I got two options for you first thing tomorrow."

"Bet! Holla back." L. Said.

It was still light outside so going to my stash house was out. I wanted to get everything in order for tomorrow. I went in the house and headed straight to my room and turned both my TV and radio on to waste time until the sun went down. Besides I was trying to avoid contact with my Dad. We ain't been on good terms lately. About an hour later my brother comes running to my room like a wild man.

"Boy stop running in my fucking room like you crazy!" I yelled.

"Daddy knows you cuss like that?" said Troy.

"Man I'm grown."

"No you ain't Russ."

"Troy what do you want and where you been at?"

"I was at Ron's house chillin'. You get my sneaks?"

"Damn I forgot, but here go get them tomorrow yourself." I handed him a hundred dollar bill.

"Thanks Russ!"

"You're welcome. Is Dad here?"

"Yeah, he's upstairs with Mommy."

"Does he know I'm here?"

"I think so Russ, why?"

"Nothing, just asking. Aight, get out before I take my money back. Come back later on."

"Aight, bye you punk ass" as he ran out laughing.

My little bro was crazy as hell, always begging, but what are little brothers for. I set my alarm clock for 12:30am so I could get up and go to my stash house. I ran upstairs to grab a bite to eat and jetted back down stairs. I was trying to avoid everybody, so I turned my ringer off on my phone and relaxed in my bed until I fell asleep. I awoke with a hard-on because I had to pee bad as hell. I glanced over at my alarm clock."Shit" I yelled. It was 2:30am. Why hadn't my alarm sounded? I checked it and found out I set it for 12:30pm instead of am by mistake. I quickly got dressed ad headed out of my window with keys in hand. I decided to take the window because I didn't want to chance waking anybody with the back door. Halfway out the window I had to climb back in because I forgot my flashlight and lunch box. I grabbed both and headed back out. Once I got the lock off the door I hustled up the 3 flights of steps, almost tripping twice due to how dark it was in there. "It's dark as a muthafucka in here" I said in a whisper. "Here we go" I said while opening a box filled with money. It was only 30 grand in that one, so I put it neatly in the lunch box and went to another box that was 10ft away. I grabbed 20 grand and closed the box. I put the lock back on the door, checked my surroundings and went the fuck back home.

I couldn't wait until tomorrow. I stayed up for the remainder of the night until I heard T. beeping his horn for me out front of my house. I would usually eat, but I figured I'd eat at Burger King once T. dropped me off. I gave T. the lunch box and told him to be safe, as we drove to Northeast to drop me off. Once we got in front of the school, I got out the car and told him to call me when he got back. I gave him a peace sign and he pulled off. As 3rd period class began, I decided to not even go. I was too anxious about being a rich man than dealing with my gay-looking Algebra teacher, plus I was hungry. As I exited the school on my way to Burger King, I was thinking why the fuck didn't L. meet me today to get these funky ounces. "Shit L., you incompetent son-of-a-bitch" I said to myself. Soon as I got to the corner of the school, I was blocked off by truancy police. I should've ran...

Chapter 10

Besides doing well at Shell Cross and being less than 250 points away from completing my gold card, I felt like the biggest ass on the planet Earth. Everything bad seemed to be happening too fast. Not only would I not be returning to Northeast, but T. hadn't returned with weed or money. I haven't heard from him in 2 weeks. It was already the end of May and the school year was closing in. How and where would I sell the weed anyway? Northeast was my outlet. With that out of the picture I had to think fast on a way to get rid of 250 pounds. Where in the fuck was T. with $50,000 of my fucking bread? "I knew it! How the fuck could you do this to ya young boy?" I said to myself in disgust. T. was like the older brother I never had. I felt betrayed. If I ever saw T. again I was leaving him wherever I found him. Whatever love I had for T. was gone. I just had to get a gun.

Chapter 11

Two blocks away from the house was a shady used car lot where money could get you anything. I was looking for something simple and clean. Carlos, the Spanish owner, had everything you needed. Everything if you know what I mean. When you left this lot, you had to double check everything. It was no telling what was stashed in your ride. One minute you're the proud owner of a new Honda, next you're being surrounded by State Troopers and K-9 dogs because you had a brick stashed in your glove box.

"Yo Carlos" I yelled.

"Hey Russ my friend, how's it going?"

"Ain't shit man. Look I need a whip, like right now man. What you got?"

"Well how much are you trying to spend poppi?"

"I got like $6500. Oh I need a .40 cal too."

"Wait a minute poppi. I can get you the car. But I don't know nuttin' 'bout no guns"

"Cut da shit Carlos. You've known me since pampers. Don't play me!"

"Okay poppi, but you gotta keep ya mouth shut."

"Aight. I need you to hook up the paperwork for me too Carlos."

"No problem poppi. You see something you like?"

"Yeah. I like that midnight blue Taurus wagon. Can you do it for $6500?"

"Poppi, give me $7000 and I'll throw the burner in and take care of the paperwork. Deal?"

"Deal! Just let me test drive it to my crib to grab the money."

"Hurry back poppi."

I fell in love with the car as soon as I pulled off the lot. It had leather and a sun roof, plus the windows came tinted. Perfect young boy whip. I couldn't look for T. on foot, plus I had to move around to get my hustle back in order. Walking was yesterday's news. 15 minutes later I was back with the money and fully in love with my wagon. "Carlos, we good to go baby." I said. He replied, "Give me 10 minutes poppi." I sat in the car and played the radio until Carlos finished up. Jadakiss was being interviewed on Power 99, so I turned it up and reclined my seat. Tap-Tap-Tap. Carlos was tapping on the window with all my paperwork in hand along with my gun in a paper bag.

"Everything is good poppi." he said. "I appreciate it Carlos." I said as I handed him a Nike box with $7000 in it. As he walked away I looked in the bag to see my new toy. I checked the clip and he even loaded it for me. Wasn't nuttin' like a husky cromeboy. I checked out my new paperwork. The info read: Randy Forester, whoever the hell that was. I was getting ready to joy ride when I got a page from Tasha. I decided to ride over there instead of calling. I had to start giving my cell a rest. My bill was high as shit last month. I pulled up outside of Tasha's window beeping my horn.

Tash pulled the screen up and asked, "Russ who's car you got?"

"Baby this my car. I just got it. You like it?"

"Yeah it's nice boo. I need you to come up, it's important."

"Aight let me park." I yelled up. "Tash, where you at?" I said as I entered the apartment.

"I'm in the bathroom Russ. Come here."

"Nah. I'll wait to you come out stink butt."

"Boy don't even play. Come here." I stepped foot in the bathroom and Tasha was holding a plastic stick in her hand that looked like a thermometer. "What the hell is it Tash?" I asked. "Boy I'm pregnant dummy." she said smiling. "What? How did that happen? I mean when? Ahhh never mind!" I just picked her up and kissed her on the lips. I was excited at becoming a father.

Money wasn't tight. I was hittin' niggaz off with weight from the 6 pounds I still had, but I definitely felt the loss of the Northeast operation. It was time to make something happen fast, if I planned on providing for my family. After I finished making love to Tasha, for the 3rd time, I decided to jump in the shower real quick, get dressed and take a ride in my new wheel. It was late, but so what. A black hoody, black Girbaud jeans, and black chuckas was the attire for the evening, as I slid behind the wheel of my wagon. I was heading straight with no particular destination. I decided to hit the boulevard to open the car up on the open road. The Biggie tribute was on the radio as I sang along.

"What the fuck." I said noticing this Acura to my left. It looked too familiar. Someone was loading big bags in the trunk. Their back was facing me, so I couldn't make out the person. A car horn was blasting off behind me because I had slowed down right in the middle of the boulevard. I banged a U-turn and pulled in the hotel parking lot where the car was. I hit the head lights and laid my eyes on him. It was T.

Chapter 12

I couldn't believe this nigga was back in the states
loading suit cases in the fucking trunk like he ain't have a
care in the world. I was right on his ass though, watching
every move. Suddenly my heart was filled with anger, and
my palms were itchin' to shoot. The rush I was feeling was
unbelievable. I reached under my seat and grabbed my
heat, cocked it and proceeded to walk two cars down from
his. He had walked back in the hotel, so I waited. Five
minutes later he was coming back out with two more suit
cases in hand. He was totally oblivious to my greasy ass
dressed in all black. After he closed the trunk he opened the
driver's side door and got in. Before he could close the
door shut I made my move. Hoody over my head and gun
by my side, I approached him. "Hey Russ I just cal-"
(BOOM_BOOM_BOOM) I let off three quick shots,
cutting him off mid-sentence, that riddled his chest and sent
him damn near over to the passenger seat. I felt no remorse
as I snatched the keys out the ignition and opened the trunk
to claim what was mine. I took four suit cases and one big
ass duffle bag from the trunk and sat it near the back tire, as
I went to get my wagon. I pulled up beside it and put
everything inside my hatch back.

All you heard were tires screeching as I peeled
away from the scene. My adrenaline was pumping as I sped
back to Tasha's. I double parked in front of the complex
and hustled to the door with two suit cases. I opened the
door and threw the suit cases on the living room floor and
headed back to the car. I came back to the living room with
a duffle bag over my shoulder and two suit cases in my
palms. I threw them on the floor and almost fell 'cause the

shit was mad heavy. By then Tasha was wide awake looking me in my face.

"Tasha, will you please take ya ass back in the room and shut the door please." "Russ what's going on baby?"… "Tasha please do what I said." She went back in her room while I ran back down the stairs to park the car. I parked the wagon two blocks away and stashed the smoking gun in the engine. Afterward I walked back to the complex. When I got in, Tasha was in her room still, so I put everything in the laundry closet. Tomorrow I would sort out everything. I had to check on my baby, who was crying in the room.

"Tash- baby, you alright?" I said rubbing her back. "Baby what happened? I woke up and you were gone."

"Everything is fine babe. Don't you worry about anything. Just stay healthy for our baby, you hear."

"Yes. Are you staying here tonight Russell?"

"I ain't going nowhere." My clothes hit the floor and I climbed in the bed and took it down. I was dead tired.

The following morning I awoke to an empty bed. Tasha headed out for school this morning without bothering to wake me. I ain't feel like going anyway. I could afford a day off. It was only 7:30am so she just had left anyway.

I flipped the TV on and caught last night's episode all on the news. I felt queasy in the stomach about that night and the fact that my friend was really dead from my own hands. Nevertheless, what was dome was done, plus he robbed me first. I got dressed and went to check my voice mail. My phone was off damn near the whole day yesterday. "You have four new messages, press one to play messages." I pressed #1.

"Yo Russ it's me T. hit me back." I couldn't believe what I heard. "To play your second message, press#2" I pressed 2.

"Yo Russ where you at dog? I got back man. Shit was crazy at custom that's why I took so long ... Look I ain't tryna rap too much on this phone, but I'm a be at the hotel on the boulevard next to IHop. If you don't hit me by tonight I'll get at you tomorrow. Yo Russ were back homie. Peace."

I pressed two again just to be sure. "Tonight ... We're back homie... Peace." Immediately I broke down with tears!

Chapter 13

I hurry up and drive to Broad and Wyoming to see if I could catch Tash before the yellow bus snatched them up. After all the craziness, I just wanted to be around someone comforting, even though I couldn't possibly tell her what went down. When I pull up I see Tasha crying all crazy with Jules all in her face yelling and pointing his finger. I parked the car and suddenly all the anger and adrenaline I felt last night at the hotel resurfaced.

I jumped out the car with my burner in the pocket of my hoody and walked quickly to Jules, getting in between them. I held Tasha away with one arm and Jules with the other. This crazy nigga was still cursing and pointing like I never existed. I pulled my .40 out and smacked him right in his face with it. Blood and teeth went everywhere, as he fell backwards. I grabbed the back of his head and shoved the nose of my gat down his throat, causing him to choke. All the while with a terrified look in his eyes. To be so big, Jules was a cold pussy. "Muthafucka, if you ever disrespect my girl again, you die bitch." "Russ please baby… Lets just get out of here." Tasha cried.

"Tash you cool?"

"Yes baby. Please don't kill him. He ain't worth it baby."

"Jules- today must be your lucky day faggot." I said, then took the gun out his mouth. I took Tasha by the hand and put her in the car and we were gone.

"Look Tash- forget school today- it's Friday anyway. We'll go back Monday , alright?"

"Alright. "

"You sure you're okay?"

"Yes baby. I just wanna go home."

"Aight , but what was all that about anyway?"

"I don't know. I get to the bus stop, I see Jules and I tell him that we live together and I'm pregnant. Then the nigga just snapped, calling me all types of whores and shit."

"I shoulda killed that nigga. Baby I think he liked you. All that brother and sister stuff was bogus to me ... Ever since he found out about us he's been acting funny towards me."

"Baby I don't know what his problem is. If he did like me he had me fooled."

"Yeah whatever ... From now on stay away from dude before I wind up merking his goofy ass."

Tasha was still teary eyed as we pulled in front of our apartment. I told her once we got in to go clean herself up in the bathroom. Once we entered, she headed towards the bathroom and I toward the laundry closet. I had to make sure of what was in those suit cases and duffle bag.

"Bing" I said, as I opened up the first suit case which revealed what appeared to be 100 pounds of weed that was compressed and wrapped in ten individual blocks. The same was revealed in the other three suit cases and duffle bag. 500 pounds in all. I was ecstatic, but at the same time I felt like crap for murdering my good friend and partner. I should've known better thinking he would try and get over on me.

"But what's done is done" I said to myself. Jay-Z said it best, "Gotta learn to live with regrets." I put everything back in the suit cases and bag and made plans to take it to the stash spot later on tonight.

Suddenly my chain of thoughts were broken by a hail of screams coming from the bathroom. "Oh please god no. Nooo! Nooo!" I could here Tasha pleading and crying in the bathroom. The door was locked though. "Tash baby open the door." No answer, just cries and screaming. "Open the door now Tash!" ... BOOM! I couldn't take it any longer

I broke down the door with my shoulder. What I saw looked so horrible and grotesque. Tasha was squatting over the toilet and blood was everywhere She was hemorrhaging badly. From watching too many episodes of E.R, I could pretty well determine that I was about to lose my unborn child and possibly the mother. I wasn't about to sit and wait for an ambulance so I ran and got a sheet from the bedroom and wrapped her up in it. I threw her over my shoulder, put her in the back seat of the car and was headed for Germantown Hospital's Emergency Room.

The doctors took her away in a wheel chair as I waited in the lobby like a helpless puppy. An hour and a half later I noticed the doctor returning to speak with me with that oh so familiar expression.   The kind where it's all bad news. I stood up to meet the doc, with hopes for the best, but I always expected the worse. "Sir your girlfriend is fine, but she lost an extreme amount of blood, causing her to lose the baby. She was 8 weeks along. Right now we have her heavily sedated, so unfortunately she's incoherent at this time. It would be best if you left and came back tomorrow, so she can rest. Sir ... Sir ... are you okay?"

I was devastated. My plans on being a good daddy were gone now and my girl was in an operating room all alone. A tear rolled down my cheek as I stood there with a blank look on my face, staring at nothing in particular.

"Sir, I'm very sorry." The doctor said, before returning to the operating room. Life sucked at this point. The world will definitely pay for these fucked up cards I was being dealt. I grabbed my keys and headed home.

Chapter 14

Tasha stayed in the hospital for a week to follow. I was there with her every day. After school I headed straight to the hospital and that's where I left every morning. I had packed clothes and everything to stay at the hospital. My baby needed me and I was gonna be there for her. I was the only real family she had or the only real family that cared.

It was only a week of school left and Mrs. A had submitted my forms to the Department of Education along with my recommendation of schools I wanted to attend in the fall. Deep down I was happy, but by no means was I in the mood for celebration. I saw Jules from time to time passing through the school hallways. He still didn't get his broken teeth fixed. He avoided eye contact with me as we passed. Oh well he brought that on himself I thought.

Back at the hospital, Tasha was back to normal. She was to be released this afternoon. I'd brought her a change of clothes also, because I knew how she felt about hospital clothes. I stopped off at a flower shop and picked up some tulips and balloons along with her favorite butter pecan ice cream to heal her spirits a bit. I figured she'd be down about the baby and all. When I walked in with the gifts I said, "Excuse me Ma'am, I was told that there was a sick woman named Tasha in here. I don't see no one sick. Could you tell me where I can find her?"

"Boy, you so silly. Stop playing." Tasha said.

"Tasha baby. What's cracking?"

"Ain't shit." She said jokingly. She was back to her old self. "Russ are those for me?" Referring to the ice cream and flowers. "They sure are, and I brought your favorite, butter pecan."

"Russ, I love you."

"I know girl, but I love you more."

I gave her everything along with her change of clothes. "You ready to bounce?"

"Boy I've been ready, I hate hospitals."

"Get dressed and we out."

As we checked out we said good bye to all the nurses and doctors. The younger nurses seemed to be on my dick a little. Girls love it when you treat your woman well because they can only imagine it being them.

We stopped home to put the flowers in water and drop our bags off. Plus we both wanted to take showers to rid us of that hospital smell. Afterward we decided to go out to dinner. I picked a Japanese restaurant on Main St. with great seafood and fillet mignon. They also cooked everything on a table/grill right in front of you. Tash loved it.

After we ate I ordered some warm saki that had us giggling like crazy. It's like warm liquor, but not as potent. It's good though. When we were done I decided to head over to Mainly Shoes, which was only a few stores down. I got her a pair of Miu-Miu sneakers that she liked, and I got a black pair of D.J. Pliners. It was there in the store that I told her that both our teachers said we really didn't have to finish the remaining week of school out due to the circumstances, plus our work was sufficient for the school year. I also explained to her that my recommendation was submitted to the Department of Education and chances were I'd be attending a new school in the fall.

She said she was happy for me but her body language told me different. I didn't understand her. What was the big deal; we were living together for god's sake. Oh well, she'd just have to be mad 'cause I was definitely getting out of Shell Cross. Although the staff was cool and Tasha was there I never really felt as though I belonged.

When we got back home I threw our bags on the living room floor and headed to the bedroom. I was exhausted. I took my boots off and stretched out on the bed. Tasha laid in my arms on top of me. Some days I really just enjoyed holding her in my arms. Today was one of them.

I laid there deep in contemplation mode, trying to figure out my next move as far as getting rid of this work I had. I had 500 brand new pounds to move with no major outlet. I had to get on the ball. What good was it having work if you couldn't move it. You were really in the way if you couldn't make something happen with that much weed. Once again, I had to step my hustle game up.

Chapter 15

I was sitting in the apartment going over my plan to get this paper. School was officially out and I had the apartment for the majority of the day. I had sent Tasha out the crib this morning to do some summer job hunting. She was starting to get on my damn nerves lately with all this laying up under me shit. This would give her something constructive to do with her day while allowing me to take care of business. Part one of my plan was already done. I had staked out this strip that was located a few blocks away from Northeast High School.

The strip was made up of a local arcade, a pool hall, and movie theatre. All were popular amongst the high school kids. In fact a lot of kids from all parts of the city were coming there. It was a fun place to hang and most importantly, get high.

There were already a few kids that lived in the neighborhood who were selling. Most of them heard of me from my days at Northeast, so it wouldn't be hard for them to come to my terms once things got rolling. I didn't plan on making them stop hustling, they just had to get down with my plans. Besides, my shit would be organized anyway, allowing all parties to eat.   Right now things were working recklessly out there. That would soon change.

I rounded up a couple young boys from my neighborhood to put this plan in motion. I also got in touch with my two white boys from Northeast and L. Both pretty much knew how I liked to run things so they would be useful. Plus they all had hoopties to get around in.   I instructed everyone to meet me at Wister Playground to go over the plan. We just had to wait on Gunter and Jeremy (my two white boys) to pick up Mike, Ron and Steve, (the three cats that were hustling up there already) I wanted everybody together so they would know who they were working with.

Once everyone got there (eleven in total) I explained that they would be divided in groups according to their locations. Each group would have a captain, who would be responsible for making sure that they had product ready to be moved. At the end of each day all money would be handed over to the captains, who would then report to me. Only the captains were to page me in case of work shortage. "Gunter, you take three soldiers with you and set up shop at the arcade. Jeremy you do the same at the pool hall, and L. you take two with you to the movie theatre." I said.

Mike went with L., Ron with Jeremy, and Steve with Gunter. This way since they all knew the location already they would be helpful. Plus I wanted to keep them separated in case they started to form a plot against me.

I instructed everyone that they were to operate from 8:00am to 10:30pm when everything shut down. All sales were to be conducted in the back parking area of the buildings. Nothing was to be done out front, it was in too much of a plain view. I had already spoken with one security guard from each spot who agreed to supply me info of any raids or misconduct of my workers. For that I promised each of them $200 a week. They were more than happy.

"Also guys. Every Sunday morning at 7:00am we will have a meeting in this same playground to discuss any changes or problems. Are there any questions?" No one spoke. "Captains, I will give you a call tomorrow. Everything goes down tomorrow. Aight fellas you can roll. Hey L. let me holla at you in private. "

"What up Russ", L. said.

"Look dog, I really don't trust Gunter and Jeremy too much. You got an extra $100 a day if you keep ya eyes and ears on them dog."

"No problem Russ. It's done."

"My man. I'ma make you rich dog. I'll call you tomorrow."

See L. was cool, but I didn't trust him either, that's why I made the same deal with Gunter and Jeremy. I had everybody watching everybody. I was always taught that in the land of the sharks you gotta be a fucking whale.

Once I left my crew I headed to my safe house to bag up a few pounds for tomorrow Five hours and twenty-eight minutes later I had bagged up 10 pounds of that sticky icky. "$1,500 a pound. Let's see times 10 pounds. That's $15,000 worth in dimes and twenties. I had no intentions on selling any weight. I still hadn't found a supplier yet, so every dollar had to count. Every bag would be distributed equally. Everyone would be paid the following morning. Each person stood to make $22,727 in less than two months' time. Me on the other hand stood to make a half a million.

As days turned into weeks, business was doing well. I had a vision this spot would do numbers. We sold 10 pounds a day on an average. That was $10,000 profit every single day. My workers couldn't complain either, they were making close to $500 a day.   That was better than any summer job I knew of. My only problem was I had no supplier and we were moving the shit too fast. I decided to give Carlos a try.

Chapter 16

I was headed towards Carlos' auto lot to try my hand at finding a new weed connect. See Carlos was low key. He never got really dressed up, never hung out and always drove a humble looking vehicle. But I knew better. Whether you like it or not the streets talk, so I knew Carlos was major.

He was born and raised in Puerto Rico, so he had a direct line from his peoples back home. Carlos mostly moved coke. I just hoped he could get weed for me. I pulled up in front of the lot beeping my horn early that morning. I wanted to catch him early when he first opened.

My hope would be that it wasn't crowded so we could rap. Carlos came out patronizing his homeland. He had on some flip-flops, raggedy jeans and an "I love Puerto Rico t-shirt."

"Buenos Dias Russ"

"Buenos Dias Carlos."

"Is the car okay poppi?"

"Yeah, yeah, the car is just fine. I need to talk to you about something else though. Is there somewhere we can talk?"

"My office. Come."

We walked to his office and I explained to him my dilemma. Come to find out he knew a whole lot about me and my operations. I guess he had his ears to the streets also. We got right down to business. "Carlos, I'm looking to buy at least 500 pounds of marijuana maybe more if you can make something happen.

"I'll have to see what I can do ... I really don't deal with marijuana. It's too bulky, and not enough money involved. You understand my friend."

"Wait right here Carlos." I said. I came back with a duffle bag I had in my trunk. Inside was $75,000 cash. I wanted to show him I was serious. I opened the bag to show him the money. "Russ that's a lot of money to be riding around with poppi." Carlos said in his best Puerto Rican accent. "Yeah, yeah, yeah. Can we do business Carlos?"

"Like I said, I don't do marijuana. But here's what I can do for you. I have a shipment supposedly coming in two days. I can ask my connection if he can do 1000 pounds if you can handle it. If he can and you can handle it, then I guess we can do business. " "Fair enough Carlos ... Call me."

I thought Carlos was bullshitting 'cause he called me in three days instead of two. When he called I was more than ready. "Hey Carlos what's going on?"   I said into the phone. "Everything is a go poppi. Meet me at the lot."

I got to the lot in fifteen minutes. "So Carlos what's good." "What's good is this. My supplier gave me 1000 pounds of marijuana as a gift for what I spent with him for coke.   Now I will give you it for ... let's say $100,000. Is that okay? I just want to get rid of it." "Carlos that's beautiful. I'll get the money right now."

"Before you go take this key. It's to a storage garage on Washington Lane. That's where they are. They're stacked in crates, weighing 250 pounds each. You'll need a truck so you must get moving because I need everything out by this week." "No problem Carlos. It's done!"

"Look poppi. It's too much trouble for me to be bringing all that weed back. From now on you need to make arrangements to pick it up from Miami. I cannot do it again." Carlos said sternly.

What he said was a minor problem, but I would take care of that. I went and borrowed a pickup truck from this neighborhood from a smoker named Vick. Vick would do just about anything for $50. I loaded everything up in the truck and headed back to Carlos's to drop off his cash.

That night I had a meeting with my crew. I explained to them that I expected everyone to try and pick up the pace. We were halfway through the first 500 pounds, but things had to pick up if I was going to move 1000 more pounds every month. "Listen up everyone. From 8:00am to 12:00pm all $20 bags go for $15. This should help pick things up a bit." After I explained that I went over the books with my captains and everything was straight.

I had to think about expanding since my quantity picked up. I was expecting to be a millionaire in a few months. For weeks my business was ridiculous. My spots looked like a carnival outside, that's how many cars and people were out. I also took good care of my peoples. I bought all my captains Chevy Tahoes to ride around with their crew. It was lovely. I had money out my ass.

My stash house was filled with paper. I used to stop by my parents' house to hit my brother with money, but that's about it. My dad wouldn't accept my money. We really had nothing to talk about besides that. He almost shit his pants when he found out that I went down to his bank and paid his car off.

I was definitely running through the stuff faster than I'd expected. I was moving 25 pounds a day. Life was great. My only problem was that I was expected to re-up in less than 5 days and I had no one to go get it. I decided to call my cousin Ashley who was home for her summer break from college. She went to a university out in Florida. She was going to school for commercial law.

She was a pretty ghetto girl with a mind of a genius, not to mention a nice body. She would make some lucky man happy. Too bad I was over protective. I felt bad about involving her, but my time was running short. I knew she'd be down. Deep down she was a fucking rider, so I called her. "Hello"

"Yo Ashley! What up girl?" "Who dis, little cuz?"

"Girl ain't nuttin' about me little. Especially my pockets." "You silly boy! What up?"

"I need you to do something for me." "Whatever you need."

"Aight come on over. You still remember where I told you I lived?" "Yeah ... How's Tasha doing? That's my girl."

"She's cool. Oh yeah did I tell you she's pregnant again?" "Boy… Hell no, you know you ain't tell me shit." "Well she is. Almost two months. We're excited." "Boy I'm on my way."

Chapter 17

When I saw Ashley get off the bus I flagged her down while I was sitting in my car. I didn't want to discuss anything in the house with Tash there. The less she knew the better off she'd be if she were ever questioned by the law.

Ashley spotted me and got in on the passenger side. "What up 'lil cuz?" "Ash what I tell you about that little cuz shit" I said jokingly.

"Look Ash here's the situation. I need you once a month to make a pick up for me in Miami. You'll be riding by limo to and from. It's four crates to be picked up. Put them in the limo and come back. You do that for me you got $10,000, plus I'll buy you a car. I hate seeing you ride the bus. What do you say?"

"Let me see. Go pick it up. Come back. Get ten stacks. Sounds easy, I'm in."

"Good, I'll fill you in on the particulars the day of."

"So Russ you happy to be becoming a father again?" Ashley asked. "Shit yeah girl. And now that you've decided to make these trips for me, life couldn't be better." "Let me get up in here and see how my girl Tash is doing."

I thought it was funny how cool Ashley and Tasha were being even though they never met. They both only seen pictures of each other. They did talk a lot on the phone. I got the bills to prove it. While Ashley went in the apartment, I stayed in the car and faded away in my thoughts. I'd come a long way since the ninth grade. Two more days it was on.

Today was the day. The first thing I did was contact Carlos to see if we were still on. He assured me that we were good to go. When I met him, he handed me a key to a storage company where I, or whoever I was sending had to go to pick the stuff up. I took the key and handed him a duffle bag filled with $100,000. That was the only part of the agreement I didn't care for. I figured he was doing me a favor so I quickly diminished any ill feelings I had. Besides Carlos had plenty of dough. He could literally wipe his ass with a $100,000. So I really couldn't trip about giving him my money up front.

The next to last thing I did was call Alli-Baba' s Limo Service to make sure my stretched hummer was ready. I've come to learn that statistics show that hearses and limos are the least likely to get pulled over by police on the highway. I was taking no chances. Once that was confirmed, I shot out to West Philly to get Ashley. I told her that if anything looked suspicious at the storage company to just leave. I also told her to get the limo driver to help put the crates into the limo.

I gave her $1,000 spending money. We headed to Alli Baba's. Everything was set to go. I handed Ashley the key and told her to be safe and call me once at the halfway point and once when she got to Florida. I gave her a hug and said, "I'll see you in a few days."

Chapter 18

While Ashley was handling my affairs out in Florida, it was business as usual in the streets of Philly. Everything was picture perfect minus a few altercations my crew had with some local street punks that tried to strong arm my team. See my crew wasn't violent. Their objective was to get money, so when I heard about this little setback, I immediately nipped it in the bud. Come to find out these punks were from the Logan section of Philly. What they thought would be a sweet come up turned out to be a very harsh lesson for them. They had no idea that they were violating a quarter million dollar a week weed strip. If they did they would've though twice.

I already had my money well invested. My old head barber Samir, well he wasn't always a barber. He used to be a cold gangster back in the day. He also used to rap, so he was cool with niggaz throughout the city , especially an up and coming rap group from the Richard Allen Housing Projects in the North Philly section. Their old head, Raddic from 12th street was a cold gangster too. Raddic didn't rap though. That crazy nigga just bodied niggaz all day. Ironically, he was one of the nicest men you could meet. When Samir and the boys from Richard Allen used to record demos in local basements, I would be right there with my young ass. I had to be like 8 years old then.

Me and Raddic kind of clicked on some big brother and little brother shit. The rest is history. He's a life time friend. Only thing now is Raddic is, well let's just say he never changed completely.   Since I've been doing my thing I decided to have Raddic and his team of young boys on standby for any drama. I paid them a few grand a month whether they put in work or not.

See these young boys of his didn't hustle, all they did was smoke weed and kill shit. Period! They actually like that shit. I really didn't need those type dudes hustling for me, so I decided to use them for their talent. Murder and mayhem. I called Raddic. Yo Raddic, what's up baby?"

"Who dis, 'lil Russ?"

"Yeah nigga it's me"

"Damn nigga I ain't hear from you in a minute. What you too rich to hit a nigga"

"Nah man. I just been busy tryna put shit together dog. You know you gotta do shit ya self if you want it done right."

"Yeah don't I know it."

"Look Raddic, I need ya crew tonight." "Why what up?"

"Some dumb ass cats out Logan tryna come between me and my money machine"

"Say no more, it's done. Just let me hit my man from up Logan to make sure he don't know these fools already. I'm a call you back"

"Aight man. Hold up. Listen…. When this shit go down, I don't want them killed, just make sure they don't walk again"

"Damn, that ain't no fun man"

"Dog just listen with your crazy ass, no homicides please." "Alright man. But let me know if you change your mind"

"I won't. But hey, did your little homies like those gifts I gave them?" "Yeah man them niggaz love the shit out of you. You like the Philly robin hood nigga."

"Ha, ha, ha. You silly man. Stop flattering me."

"I'm serious dog. And they wear those Techno Marine watches every single day."

"That's good, that's why I brought them. Just make sure now that they all got watches that they be on time. 10:30 it's going down.

"Done" We hung up.

L. gave me the low down about the Logan boys. They would show up at 9:30pm and shake down whoever they thought had paper on them. It was four dudes in all, and they were doing this for three days straight. It never struck my attention because my money never came up short. Never! What did bother me was that no one told me sooner. When I asked L. why, he told me that he was embarrassed to tell me. I wouldn't have been that mad though. I knew my crew wasn't gangsters. They know how to sell weed in an organized manner. So that's what I paid them to do. I would never make them do something out of their character. That's how fuck ups happen. I always remembered that saying. My old head from a nearby housing project on Roberts Ave. schooled me to that rule. That's why at 10:30pm all this shit would cease.

At nine twenty I parked and positioned my car so I could see the events that would take place. I called L. and the others and told them that when they come, to give them the money. They all thought I was crazy, but none rebutted my request. That's what I loved about my crew. They listened.

9:30 on the dot and the four stooges came walking up with their best gangsta faces on and street apparel. They were so obvious. If they weren't they would of been harder to spot. That's the problem with fake tough guys. You spot them before they spot you. I just hoped they stuck to that gangsta shit once those shells got to flying. Nine times out of ten they would fold. Most do.

I called Raddic and told him to have his young boys meet me.   I made Raddic stay home. I didn't need him out there killing everybody. He was pissed, but he agreed. 30 minutes later a dark brown Astro minivan pulled up beside me. I got out and jumped in the van. It was my five favorite young boys. 'lil Stevey, 'lil Gary, 'lil Nate, 'lil 2 Pac (he had a bald head and swore he was 2 Pac) and the craziest of all, 'lil Pooh. 'Lil Pooh had plenty of bodies under his belt, but never was even questioned for one.

He was a smooth nigga, sort of a pretty boy. But this little nigga put that work in. I liked him the best. Quiet and low key. These little niggaz were armed to the teeth. The van was loaded with two AR-15s, two .44 Smith & Wesson revolvers, three .40's and three husky ass four pounds.

"I'm glad y'all niggaz could make it on time." I said.

They all held their wrists in the air and said in unison, "And you know it!"revealing their watches. These 'lil niggaz could be funny at times. I got right down to tactics. "Look y'all. You see them four niggaz right over there?" I said as they shook their heads yes. "That's them over there by the arcade." One of the four boys was robbing Gunter. They probably did this to the other two spots as well.   I noticed the other three assholes flashing heat on Gunter's soldiers. They looked scared as shit. My thoughts were interrupted by my cell phone ringing. I answered it in a hurry.

"Hello who dis?" "Yo it's me Raddic. I got the low down on our four little thieves." "What's the deal?" I asked.

"Well my man from Logan said he knows the niggaz, but they ain't with his crew.   In fact one of them niggaz ran up in one of his dope houses and stole $15,000, so he would very well like them taken care of too.   He's pretty sure it's the same guys from the description you gave me."

"Yo Raddic good looking. They robbin' my crew right now. Too bad it'll be their last job." I hung up. I got back on the phone and called Jeremy "Hello Jeremy. Look, they're on their way. Do what I told you."

The plan was to only hold $1000 on them and to act scared as shit. This way they would think it was sweet and roll out soon after. I wanted no altercations out in front of my spots. Once they got Jeremy, like clockwork they moved in on L. I immediately called everyone and told them to leave in ten minutes. Just like I instructed, ten minutes they all piled in their Tahoes and rolled out. I turned to my other young boy in the van. "Hey did Raddic tell y'all there is to be no killing?"

"Yes he told us Russ. That's why I brought these too" Pooh said, holding open a duffle bag filled with metal bats and lead pipes. "Good, you guys are on point. Remember nothing is to go down in front of here. Matter fact, follow them back to the hood." "We got it dog"

Just then the four guys decided to leave. One of the guys decided to make a few weed sales before they left. I took that as time to get back in my wheel. Once he was finished, they got in their car and headed towards the boulevard.

"Look at these fools four deep in one car. This should be easier than planned" I said in the car as I proceeded to follow behind my young boys who were following them. My young boys were unaware that I was following them. I had to make sure this was done right.

They tailed their marks perfectly, not tagging too close to be spotted. Both vehicles turned right on 9th street and the boulevard. While shots immediately rang out, I kept straight then made a U-turn and parked on the other side of the Boulevard. What I saw was happening so fast. These 'lil niggaz came for war.

"BLLLLAT, BLLLLAT, BLLLLAT.... BOOM, BOOM, BOOM... BLLLLAT"

That's all I was hearing as I seen the Astro van cut in front of their car, letting off about a hundred shots from the sliding door. They lit the whole bottom of their car to shreds, causing them to get out and run for cover. A few shot back, which only caused little 2 Pac to go into a frenzy. "Oh you pussy's want war!" he spat, as he stood on the hood of the van spraying his AR-15 like hair spray. 'Lil Nate was right beside him with his, letting mad shells drop

75

from a hundred round drum. 'Lil Stevey and Gary sat in the van shooting off .45's and .40's with both hands. All the shots were aimed below the waist, even though a few niggaz got hit in the arm when they opened fire on the car. When one reloaded, the other kept bussing. All you heard was guns cracking and screams as the bullets ripped through their asses and legs. These dudes would never walk again, let alone wear shorts ever again. Three of the four even dropped their guns when those shells got to flying. They were too busy running and trying not to get hit.

Two were running and trying to escape the wrath, while the other two lay in their own blood, moaning on the concrete. Pooh, who was driving, jumped from his seat with two black .44 revolvers in hand and chased them. "Don't run now bitches" "BOOM! BOOM! BOOM! BOOM!" I was watching this kid run towards them while bussing his gun. It was like something out of a god damn movie, I thought. He hit both of them in the shoulder which sent them flying forward on their face. He stood over top of them. "Please don't kill me man. Please!" they said, begging for some leniency. Pooh just smiled and emptied his gun in their legs. As they laid there screaming, Pooh reached in their pants pocket and withdrew the money they'd stolen.

"Look you dumb muthafucks. You see this money. Next time you die with it. Stay from up the Northeast pussys." He then threw the money in their faces. Suddenly the van pulls up and out jumps the crew. They all had bats and pipes in hand. They pounded the shit out of them until they all fell unconscious. My crew ran back to the van laughing. They sped away heading towards North Philly.

I'd seen what I came for. I drove away and went home. The message was out. NORTHEAST WAS STILL MINE.

Chapter 19

As I made my way home I was tripping on why Ashley didn't call me, she should have been at the halfway point by now. I decided not to worry. I parked my car two blocks away as usual. I got in the habit of doing this just in case a nigga tried to follow me. He would have to follow me two extra blocks. This way I would see everything before I went in my house. I also got in the habit of walking with my gun at my side while going to the apartment. Better paranoid than paralyzed.

When I got in, Tasha was in the bedroom laying down eating ice cream and watching old "Martin" re-runs. Tasha's stomach was really starting to show. I thought as I rubbed her tummy. "You miss me Tash?"

"You know I did Russ." "Hey did Ashley call?" "No why?"

"Nah it ain' t nuttin'"

Just then, Tasha started playing with my zipper. "Hold up baby. Let me take a quick shower. I've been rippin' and runnin' all day."

"Well go ahead funky boy. Hurry up, mommy's hungry for that dick." I loved it when she talked like that. I ran and took a quick shower, and came back into the room with just a towel on. "Come to mommy Russ." she said, placing herself on all fours. She had on some coochie-cutter shorts and no shirt. Her C- cup titties looked so perky and delicious. I dropped my towel and let my manhood stand at attention. I walked towards her and she held her mouth

78

open so I could slide it right in with ease. She sucked the life out of me while I reached over her back and fingered her ass.

Her ass was getting fatter since the pregnancy, and it was really turning me on. I couldn't help but come in her mouth. She wasted not even a drop. I pulled out of her mouth and pulled off her shorts. Her pussy lips were swollen fat, not to mention juicy. Since she had shaved all her hair off her kitty-kat it really looked fat. I decided to taste what looked so good. I let Tasha sit on my face. Her whole ass covered my face as she grinded on it trying to come faster.

"Oooh, suck my pussy .... Oooh suck my pussy you nasty muthafucka you…. Oooh…" I could barely breathe, let alone respond back. I just kept sucking so she could come. "... Oooh baby ... I'm a come all on your face ... Uhhh ... Uhhh ... I'm coming…. I'm coming ... I'm coming!

She came all over my face. She got up and bent over right in front of me. She smacked her ass, turned around and said fuck me good. I stuck my dick in as far as I could go. I fucked her real good from the back. Her pussy was feeling extra good. If you've ever fucked pregnant pussy than you know what I'm talking about. It was feeling so good I almost came too fast, so I pulled out. I made her lay flat on her stomach.

I ran my tongue up the crack of her ass, then I slid my dick straight in her ass. Her ass felt so good and tight that I came in like ten minutes all over her ass cheeks. Tasha got up and went in the bathroom and cleaned up.

She came back with a nice warm wash cloth to wipe me down with. That was my kind of girl, always considerate. I laid there ass naked and dozed off to sleep.

I woke up to the sound of my cell phone vibrating on the night stand. Tasha was asleep next to me with her arms around my neck. I eased out of her grasp without waking her and grabbed my phone off of the night stand. I answered it and proceeded to the bathroom.

"Hello who is dis?" I asked half sleep. "It's me boy. Ashley."

"Ashley- why you just now calling? What time is it?"

"It's 3:00 in the morning, and I did call, but your voice mail kept coming on"

"So why didn't you leave a message?"

"Because nigga. I ain't feel like it. Besides I'm here right?"

"Ashley you goin' make me hurt you girl. So I see you made it. You alright?" "Yeah I'm good. We at the gas station right now though. We tryna get directions to a close hotel."

"Alright. But make sure y'all get separate rooms."

"I don't know. I was thinking about letting him shack up with me. He's kind of cute, you know."

"Girl don't fucking play with me. Business first. Do that shit on your own time."

"Boy I know. I was just playing anyway. He is cool though" "Well you and Mr. Cool man just stick to the script aight?"

"Aight. We'll be going to the storage spot early tomorrow morning. I'll call you then. Bye lil cuz."

"What I tell you about callin' me littl-?" She hung up on me in mid-sentence. That girl was something else. Now that I knew she was alright I could relax.

Chapter 20

7:00 the following morning Ashley and the limo driver checked out of the hotel and made way to the storage company. The number on the key said 14, so Ashley told the manager at the front desk that she would be needing garage 14. He buzzed the gate to allow the limo to roll in front of garage #14. Ashley went in by herself to see if everything was in place. "Yep just like Russ said. Four big ass crates"

She signaled for the manager again to get some sort of pulley or wagon to pull the heavy ass crates out. The manager instructed one of his employees to help out. He came back with some sort of flatbed on wheels. Ashley and the employee worked together to put the crates onto the flat bed. When she was bending over to lift the crate, she looked between her legs and found the limo driver staring at her goods. "You see something you like?"

"Sort of" he said.

"Since you wanna eye ball a bitch ass all crazy, why don't you help with these humungous ass crates."

"It ain't nuttin' ma." He helped load all four crates onto the flatbed and then into the limo. Tasha called me out of breath while I was in the kitchen eating a bowl of raisin brand, watching the news. "Hello" "Yeah, Russ it's me. Everything is a go."

"Word! That's what's up. So I guess I'll see you around 12 tonight" "You sure will. Tell Tasha I said hi."

"Well she's at work right now, you know she got that job at the cheese cake factory up King of Prussia."

"For real! I guess I'll holla when I get back. Yo Russ." "What?"

"Listen to this. Click!" She hung up in my ear. That girl was crazier than me sometimes. I finished my cereal and headed out the door to meet my crew. I had to pick my paper up from last night. I was already running a half hour late.

When I got to Wister Playground, Gunter, Jeremy, and L. were already waiting. "Sorry I'm late fellas." I said. I hated to be late especially when I expected my crew to be on time. I always felt you had to lead by example.

"Is everything straight yall?" I asked.

"Yeah everything is cool." L. reached and threw me a book bag with $28,000 in it. $3,000 too much, which only meant that the money they got robbed for, they took that from their earnings. I sat on the bench and counted the stacks, all neatly placed in $1000 stacks.   I loved my crew. They were loyal dudes. I took three stacks and tossed it to them. "Yall keep that"

"Thanks Russ!"

"Don't thank me it's yours." Then I gave them each $500 more. "Go buy y'all girls something nice, you cheap bastards." Jeremy laughed and said, "shiiiit, I don't love them hoes." I started laughing because for a white boy he had a good Snoop Dogg impression.

L. looked at me and stated, "What about last night? We still good?" "Nigga you seen the news, of course we're good."

The 11:00 news reported live from 9th street where the reporters said that "4 young black men were seriously shot and beaten last night on 9th and Roosevelt Boulevard. Their vehicle was apparently gunned down. There were no witnesses. When police arrived on the scene the victims were bleeding badly from the leg area and unconscious. They were immediately taken to Temple Hospital and were listed in critical condition. No weapons were found at the scene. I'm 'Robert Blakely, reporting live from Logan Philadelphia- Channel 6."

My young boys must've picked up their weapons before breaking out. I must have missed that, then again I was looking from the other side of the boulevard. "Everything is back to normal." I said assuring my crew.

I looked down at my watch, it was five minutes to nine. "Y'all running late." I spent the rest of the morning looking for a better apartment. I found a nice house for rent in Conshohocken, PA. It was 15 minutes outside of Philadelphia. It was a nice three bedroom with a finished basement and two car garage. It was beautiful. I knew Tasha would love it, so I decided I was going to surprise her with it. I just had to find someone willing to use their credit to get it for me. All that ghetto cash shit wasn't working there. I figured I'd give Ashley's credit a try.

At least she had credit and whatever her credit didn't provide I would make up with cash.   It sounded like a plan.

It was 4:00pm by the time I left from looking at the house. I rode to King of Prussia, to pick Tasha up at her job. It was only 15 minutes from Conshohocken, so I would be there at 5:00 get her. I walked around the King of

Prussia mall for like 45 minutes just to waste time. I wound up buying me and Tasha outfits from the Louis Vitton shop, then I breezed through the Gap and got us both underclothes. I didn't feel like going home, so I decided to check into a nearby hotel. Three bags and $1000 later I was leaving. I threw the bags into the trunk and drove in front of the Cheese Cake Factory where Tasha was waiting outside for me.

"Hop in pretty lady." I said to her as I rolled the window down. She walked in front of the car and got in the passenger seat. She gave me a kiss and started flipping through my CD booklet until she found her favorite one. She popped it in and started to sing along with R. Kelly. "Let's go half on a baby, all I need is your body next to me, I'm saying oooh nah nah nah nah nah your body nah nah nah. Half on a baby…." That was my jam too, so I chimed right on in as I pulled in the valet section of the Hyatt hotel. Tasha turned the volume down on the stereo and asked me, "Russell why are we stopping here"

"Hold on for a minute Tash, I'll be right back." I ran to the front desk where Jeremy's uncle Dan was working. He allowed me to pay for a suite for the night without any I.D. I was grateful. Wasn't no way in hell any other hotel would allow a 16 year old to rent a suite. I paid for the night and tipped Dan $50. He tried to give it back, but I just walked away from him. I met the valet outside the lobby and allowed him to park my car. I grabbed Tasha, and our bags out of the trunk. "Russell why are we here baby. I'm tired and my feet hurt, I'm ready to go home."

"Baby I rented us a suite for the night and I got us both a change of clothes, underwear, tooth brush, the whole shabang."

"Well, aren't you the romantic planner."

"That be me sugar." I smiled with a wide grin. "Shall we?" I said, as I grabbed her hand and walked through the lobby.

"Yes we shall!" Tasha responded. Bags in hand, we skipped through the lobby to the elevators like we were the happiest couple alive. We got off the elevators on the 16th floor and headed to room 1604.

The room was beautifully equipped with a kitchen, living room, his and her full-size bathrooms, and a king-size bed that overlooked the city.

"This is beautiful Russell." she said as she ran to the living room and dove on the couch. I left our bags by the door and knelt down beside the couch. I took my baby's shoes off and started massaging her feet. Tasha leaned her head back and closed her eyes like she was in heaven. "Mrnrnrn that feels magnificent." Tasha moaned out.

I started up a conversation. "Hey Tasha, what do you think about quitting school, and getting your diploma through correspondence courses over the internet We can buy a computer before school starts back up."

"That don't sound bad, but I kind of like some of my friends at Shell Cross."

"Yeah I know. It's just that you'll be pregnant during the school year and you know they don't allow pregnant women to attend. That means you'll have to take off and eventually make up the work. With the correspondence courses it will be easier with the baby corning and all." "Yeah I guess your right Russell baby ... I guess so."

"I mean I ain't forcing you or anything. I was just saying."

"Nah- now that you've said it like that, it does sound like a good idea." I liked Tasha for the fact that she would always listen to good reasoning. We were perfect. I worked my way from massaging her feet to her shoulders and back. In ten minutes she was out cold. I took it upon myself to run her some warm bath water. The whole bathroom set up was cool. A big whirlpool, a walk-in shower, marble floors, and plenty of space.   It looked like a bedroom.

On the ledge of the whirlpool was a basket filled with all kinds of sponges from Bath and Body Works. I looked through all the oils and scents and decided on a peach scented bath oil. I mixed it in with the warm water until the tub was almost filled. I lit some vanilla scented candles that were on the bathroom counter. All courtesy of the Hyatt hotel. I went and retrieved our bags from in front of the door and placed them in the bedroom. Once I took the clothes out of the bag, I laid our under garments on the bed. The panties I bought Tasha were cute.   I even bought them a size smaller. Boy I couldn't wait to see her squeeze that juicy ass in them. I went back in the living room.

"Wake up sleepy head."

"Russ what time is it already?"

"It's 6:30, you've only been sleep for thirty minutes."

"What's that smell?"

"Candles… take off your clothes."

She stepped out of her dress and thongs, pulled her shirt over her head and I helped unsnap her bra as I led her to the bathroom, leaving her clothes in the middle of the floor. "Russ this is beautiful." she said, as she stepped into the whirlpool one foot at a time. She moaned as she eased her body down into the warm water. A hot bath could be very therapeutic after a stressful day. I heard someone say that on a Dove soap commercial. As she sat in the tub I leaned over the edge and kissed her on the nose, then began washing her back with a body sponge. When I finished washing her entire body she smelled just like a peach. Tasha then looked up at me and said, "Baby why are you so good to me?" Someone in her family must've really broke her self-confidence down. She never felt like she deserved anything good that I did for her. I made it my business to love Tasha the best I could.

When she asked me the question, I really didn't know what answer to give her. "Why do you love me?" I mean growing up I seen my dad always do special shit for my mom and for the most part she always seemed happy. Hell they've been married for over 16 years. Some kind of love must've been there. I figured that's what men did when they loved their lady. I guess I picked up some of my father's traits after all. I decided tomorrow I would stop by and visit my folks.

After I snapped out of what seemed like a trance, I answered Tasha's question. "Because I just love you. That's why." There was a small radio mounted on the bathroom wall. I reached and turned the power button on. "Oh shit! This is our song Tash. Right?" It was Goodbye by Aaron Hall. I started singing to my baby as I got undressed. I couldn't really sing, but I was trying to be romantic for my boo. "Bye-bye..... You said you'll never leave me. I said I'll never leave you ... But fairy tales don't always come true ... You know I'm saying bye- bye..."

I eased into the water myself. We kissed for what felt like eternity. We held each other and made love in the whirlpool. We ended up making love on the bed too. Twice. Afterwards, we laid on the bed in our nakedness. I looked at Tasha's body. She looked just as good 10 weeks pregnant as she normally did. If not better.

I thought I was thinking those words, but obviously they came out loud because a happy tear rolled down my baby's face. I kissed her tear away, as we laid next to each other until we nodded off. It was official. I was in love.

Chapter 21

I awoke to my cell phone going off. I glanced down at my watch to see the time. It's 12:30am. It was Ashley. I hit the button to talk.

"Ashley this you?"

"Yeah fool it's me. I'm back and we're good."

"Aight. Have the limo drop you off at your house. I'll meet you there." I hung up the phone and got dressed and as I was about to leave Tasha popped up.

"Russell where are you going?'"

"Nowhere. I just gotta take care of something right quick."

"You hungry Tash? Want me to bring you back something to eat?"

"No, I'm fine." she said as she rolled back under the covers. Out the door I went."

I ran through the hotel lobby and retrieved my car from valet parking. I was on my way to West Philly , but had to stop off at Wendy's to get a grub before they closed at 1:00am. When I arrived at Ashley's, she was standing outside with the limo driver chit-chatting. When I pulled up, all eyes were on me. I stepped out the car and walked over to the limo driver and extended my hand for him to shake it. "I appreciate you taking care of my cousin on that long trip." I told him. Then we helped unload the crates out of the limo and into my station wagon.

After the last crate was loaded into my ride, I handed him an extra hundred and gave him a look as to say "Alright beat it." He got the hint and bounced. "Let me find out you got a little jealousy up in you." Ashley said. "No it ain't that. It's just niggaz need to know when to roll out, that's all." I shot back.

"It's late Russ. You staying over here tonight cuz?"

"Nah, I gotta get back before Tasha swear I was out fucking." "Let me find out ya woman got it on lock."

"You don't even believe that. I wear the pants and the shirt in my relationship. She's just a good girl, so I'm trying to do right by her."

"Anyway Ashley, I'll be by tomorrow to drop your money off okay. Did you find a car you like yet?"

"Not really. I'm kind of stuck between the new Honda Accord and the convertible Seabring."

"Well hurry up and make up your mind before I change mines." "Whatever Russ."

"Hey Ash, I was thinking about throwing a big party like next week since everybody starts back to school next month, and my birthday is the 25th anyway."

"Just make sure I'm invited." Ashley said in her most ghetto-fied voice. I just laughed and said, "I'll be by to scoop you up tomorrow." I headed back to the hotel.

I eased back in my hotel room and climbed right back in the bed without waking Tasha up. The following morning we both showered and got dressed in our new outfits and walked down to the lobby where they served up an all you can eat breakfast buffet. I pigged out having four

Belgian waffles, three scrambled eggs, cheese grits, home fries, and turkey sausage. Tasha just ate a cinnamon bagel and fruit salad. Afterwards we went back to the room. I had to take a vicious shit. Eggs do it to me every time.   When I got in the room I stripped down to my boxers and headed straight to the bathroom and closed the door. "Make sure you courtesy flush boy." Tasha yelled through the door.

"Shut up girl!" I yelled back. "Hey Tash...."

"Boy don't be talking to me while you shittin."

"Girl shut up and listen. I was thinking about having a party next week, right before everybody starts back to school. My birthday is next week anyway. And I wanna stop by my parents' house. I need to squash everything with my pops. I think it's his birthday today. Matter fact it is. We can swing by and pick Ashley up on the way. Alright?"

"I'm cool with that baby. I'm off today anyway. Just hurry up, doo-doo-man. "

Twenty minutes later I was coming out of the bathroom feeling about ten pounds lighter. "Hey Tash. Don't go in there for about 35 ...45 minutes. She started laughing, while holding her nose. "Eeeelll Russ gotta dooky butt." We checked out of the Hyatt at 11:00 and drove to Ashley's. I drove through Conshohocken to take a look at a few houses on the way. Tasha thought the homes were absolutely gorgeous. I purposely drove through the section where I wanted to rent. She pointed out the exact house I was looking at the day before. "Oooh Russ, look at that house over there." "Where?" I asked dumbfounded.

"Over there. The house with the two car garage." she said pointing her finger in the direction of the home.

"That is a nice house Tash. Maybe one day we'll get it."

See Tasha knew I had money, but she didn't know I had reeeeaal paper. She also didn't know we would be living in that house soon. We got to Ashley's house around 1:30. She was sitting out on the porch when we pulled up, and started smiling when she seen Tasha in the car. We parked and got out. Tasha went running toward Ashley giving her a hug as they started their girl talk.

"Ashley girl, I love what you did to your hair." She had it in a Halle Berry type style that was cute. "Thanks girl. Oooh girl you looking big for two and a half months, but you still got your figure. You lucky."

"Thanks Ash. I don't know how long I'm gonna keep this figure once the baby comes."

"Girl you'll be fine, trust me."

"Ashley let me use your bathroom girl, I gotta pee."

"Straight upstairs on your left."

While Tasha went to the bathroom, me and Ashley talked. I handed her a wad of twenties.

"That's like $5000. I'll give you the rest later on today. I gotta stop by City Blue and pick up a gift. You know it's your uncle's birthday today?"

"Damn! Today is your pops birthday. Let me go with you so I can pick him up something too. So I take it y'all speaking again?"

She had heard about the little beef between me and my dad. "No not really. That's why I'm heading over there today. I figured I'd bring you to make it a little easier. "

"Yeah I'll go. I ain't seen your little brother in a while."

"Aight cool! We can go look at some cars while we're at it."

"Now that's what I'm talking about Russ!"

"Hey Ash... I need you to take a look at these houses for me out Conshohocken. I'm tryna rent something out there Tasha and I. But it's sort of a surprise. You think you can run your credit through?"

"Yeah, I guess. So when?"

"Probably in a couple of days."

"Aight , just let me know. Did you plan where you wanted your party at yet?"

"Yeah I had a place in mind."

"Where at?"

"It's a place on Delaware Ave behind Dave and Busters."

"What Hibachi's?"

"Yeah that's it. I heard it's real classy."

Just then Tasha came back from the bathroom. I looked at the two ladies and said, "Y'all ready to roll?" We stopped at the City Blue on Chelten Ave. Everybody knew me in the store from my sneaker days at Northeast High. I told the owner who was working behind the register today that I needed a pair of Timbs in a size 10,\ and this white linen Sean John suit in a double X along with the matching bucket hat. My dad still liked to dress like a young boy, so I had no trouble knowing what to get him. Ashley spent a buck- ten on an Akademics sweat suit while Tasha put a G-Shock watch and a T-shirt that said "I'm Not Old, I'm Just A Recycled Teenager." written on the front. The owner gave me a 15% discount, as I paid, then we left.

We walked straight past the bootleg CD table outside the store, got in the car, and headed to my big bowl of potato salad into the house. The BBQ grill was out and my dad was sitting on the steps drinking a Heineken. All the neighbors were out having a good time enjoying the food. It seemed like all eyes were on me when I pulled up. I'm not sure whether it was because everybody missed me or the fact that everyone was seeing me drive for the first time. I got out and waved to everyone. Tasha and Ashley followed behind me as I approached my dad.

We stood looking at each other for like two minutes before I decided to walk over and wish him a happy birthday. I hugged him for the first time in months. "Happy Birthday Dad. Sorry about everything. "He stayed there speechless.I could tell he was sort of happy I stopped by. Besides, I was his first boy and every day I was starting to look more and more like him. I handed him his gifts as Ashley and Tasha walked up with theirs. He accepted the gifts giving them both hugs. He then looked at Tasha strangely, because he never met her before. In fact no one in my family had met her. "Who is this pretty young lady?" my dad said. Just then my mom yelled into the living room.

"Come on outside y'all, Russell is home!" I decided to introduce everyone.

"Tasha, I'd like for you to meet my family. This is of course is my dad, my mother, that lady right there is my grandmother, we call her granny, this is my uncle Toney, and this is my 'lil brother Troy."

"Everybody this is my girl Tasha." Everyone spoke and then my granny said, "Oooh child you look pregnant." Granny had no problem speaking her mind. I said, "That's 'cause she is. Everybody I'll be the proud owner of a baby boy in February." The house was quiet until my uncle said, "Well congratulations!" Everything was cool now. The family settled down and got back to the cook out. I decided to sit and catch up on a few things with my old man.

I explained how I had finished school this year and I did well. I told him that I planned on returning to a regular school in the fall. I told him that me and Tasha had moved in together in an apartment out Mt. Airy. He told me he was happy for me, but I could move back if I needed to. I appreciated his offer, but had no plans of doing that. As we were talking, I seen my home girl Chas' across the street with her man. I waved to her. I used to have a crush on that girl back in the day. "Damn boy, what are you still moving?" What's all those big ass crates in your car?" my father said as he looked in my car from the porch. "Yeah. Those are all my clothes and some appliances I picked up." I replied.

I must've been slipping. I'd forgotten to take the crates to the stash house. That was the first thing I was doing as soon as the sun went down. Around 8:00 the sun soon faded away and I snuck out the house unnoticed while everyone was watching the "BET Awards" . I got in my car and headed to the stash house.

I had to carry all four heavy crates into the house by myself.There was no way I could carry them up a flight of steps, so I left them on the first floor. I locked up and headed back to the house, to talk to my granny about my party.

See granny was a cool ass grand mom. She loved boxing and traveling and used to take me everywhere as a kid. She was a high yellow complexion like me, and always looked ten years younger than she was, so I used to pass for her son too. The reason I had to talk to her was because Cah, one of her close friends had a son who was a radio announcer for a local radio station. I needed him to promote my upcoming party over the air. If anyone could make it happen it was granny. I convinced her to do it after promising to make the honor roll at school next year.

It was on. It was 8:45 and I almost forgot to take Ashley to the car lot, and they closed at 9:30.   I ran back to the stash house, and grabbed the bag with the $25,000 in it that I picked up yesterday from my crew. I picked up Ashley, and we stopped at a car lot on the boulevard.

I hated the boulevard because it reminded me of the night I hit T., but this was for Ashley so I dealt with it. As soon as we got there she fell in love with an all-white convertible Volvo C-70. So much for a Honda. I thought since we were the last customers, they would allow us to stay late to run Ashley's credit. When I told them I was putting down $15,000 cash they made the necessary adjustments to get her approved. At 10:02 Ashley Wade was the owner of a 2001 Volvo C-70 and it was only August of 2000.

"Damn Ash! You gotta better car than me." Matter of fact everyone one did. Even my young crew had brand new Tahoes. I was still floating around with a Taurus wagon. It didn't bother me though. I kind of preferred it that way. I was taught not to floss too hard. Never let the people under you see you doing too much better than them. It creates hate and envy. That's why I stayed humble. In this game it was a good rule. Besides, I was the one sitting on close to $600,000, and a half a ton of spinach. I was more than up.

Before Ashley got in her Volvo to leave the lot, I told her that my party was on for next week. "Yo Ash... My party is on for my birthday. For the elegant and elite only. Be there or be square."

Chapter 22

Four days before my party everything was running smoothly. My strip was still doing $25,000 a day. I couldn't be happier. I would definitely be ready next month to make that trip.

I had made all the necessary arrangements to throw my party on the waterfront at Hibachi's. The establishment cost $7,000 to rent the floor for the evening and an extra $3,000 for an open seafood bar. I also wanted to buy out the liquor bar, which consisted of Christal and Hennesy. That would be another $8,000. The club's capacity was 1,100 people and since I didn't know that many people, everyone was welcome. I just wanted to fill the room.

I passed out flyers to every hair salon and barber shop in the whole (215) area. Coby Cabe was on the air hyping my party. "This ya boy Coby Cabe. My main man Russ is throwing the biggest birthday bash of the year at Hibachi's...... That's Hibachi's on Delaware Ave behind Dave and Busters ... Christal and Henney will be flowing freely all night long ... But this is for the grown and sexy. No Timbs, sneaks, or jeans, and leave ya burners at home. Fellas come fly, and ladies come sexy, 'cause we will be holding a "Mean Shoe Contest". The lady with the best shoe walks away with five hundred dollars cash. Ladies get there before ten and you're in free. That's right. Free! So we'll see you at Hibachi's." 'Free drinks and free money that should get them there.

The night before the party, I had dropped off some money at my stash house. I kept $10,000 for the remaining balance for my party and took forty more to keep at the spot. I decided to count my stacks to see what I was really worth. I sat down and started counting. 1 ...10 ... 25 ...90 ...350...600...920...1,200. Damn, 1,200 stacks of one thousand dollars. It was a total of 1.2 million dollars. I couldn't believe I was counting a fucking million dollars in cash.   I wasn't even old enough to smoke yet. I counted it again to make sure.   Yep 1.2 million it was I grabbed my $50,000 and went home.

The day of my party was here and I was definitely excited. Tasha got up early to get her hair done with Ashley. I had to handle some business and make sure my crew was straight for the strip. Money still had to be made. I told Jeremy, Gunter, and L. to leave around 9pm and head to the party.   Mike, Steve, and Ron would take over from there, along with the rest of my crew. I wanted my captains with me. I did set something else up with the others. I told Gunter to leave his truck along with Jeremy's so they would have some wheels for the night.

I had gotten two adjoining rooms for them on the 8th floor at the Holiday Inn on City Line Avenue and had ten go-go bitches meet them there at midnight. After everything was squared away with that I went and got my hair cut and then drove down South St. to pick me and Tasha's outfits up. I got a black Gucci suit made with a matching tie, some platinum cuff links, and some Gucci loafers with a matching platinum emblem. .Tasha had gotten an all-black dress made by Amillio Pucci with spaghetti straps and some sling back heels by Christian Dior. I also bought his and her black Ferragamo sun glasses. I paid $4,000 for my suit and $500 for my loafers. Tasha's dress and shoes came to $6,000 and another $1,000 for our glasses. I almost forgot that Tasha wanted this tennis bracelet from Tiffany's jeweler. She never asked questions about my money, but she sure knew how to spend it. I bought the bracelet anyway. $8,000! I put everything in the car and headed home before I spent any more money. It was 5:00 anyway and I wanted to rest up.

I had reserved a stretched CL 500 from Alli Babba's to pick us up at the house around 11:00. When I got home Ashley and Tasha were in the apartment. They both had matching cute Halle Berry cuts. Together they looked like Halle Berry and Toni Braxton. "Can y'all get the bags out of the car for me? I'm going to lay down for a while. The limo will be here around eleven." They went to get the bags and I took a nap.

Chapter 23

The party was underway and I was sharp for my event. Me, Tasha and Ashley had slipped into the limo.

"Where to?" the driver asked. Ashley spoke up, "Sharon Hill." She had to pick up her date. I really wasn't too comfortable riding around with a nigga I didn't know, but I trusted her judgment. According to her, she had met the guy in the beginning of the Summer at a basketball game in West Philly. Ashley claims that she was walking with three of her girlfriends when this tall light skin guy approached her like a pure gentleman. They conducted small talk and eventually exchanged numbers. She liked what he seemed to be about, so she agreed to see him again, and again, and again. Now here we are picking him up today. She seemed pretty excited about this mystery guy, but I was always leery.

We got to Sharon Hill in like 25 minutes. We made a left down a small block and stopped. Out of nowhere I see my old head Raddic from Richard Allen. I roll the window down and say "Yo Raddic… What up baby?"

"Hey baby…. What's going on young buck? What brings you down these parts?"

"Ah man we just here to pick up my cousins date. You still coming to my party?"

"Yeah I'm just waiting for my ride playa." Just then Ashley says, "Wait a minute. You know Raddic?"

"Yeah why?"

"Because that's my date."

"You can't be serious." I said. I rolled the window completely down so he could see in.

"Yo Raddic do you know this girl here?" He looked closer. "Hey Ashley what you doing with my young buck Russ?"

"Boy Russ is my cousin."

"For real? Ay Russ…. I had no idea."

"Man we live in a small world … It ain't nothing, at least I know she's in good hands. Get in."

Raddic had an all-white linen shirt and slacks with some black and white Caesar Piccoitti shoes. Ashley had on a D&G mini skirt with some thigh boots by Via Spiga. We were all dressed to kill. We pulled up in front of the party and slid out of the sleek CL 500 limo. Everybody turned and stared as all four of us made our way past the crowd and into the building.

The scene looked like Vegas. Mad lights, crazy cars, and gorgeous women, all piled outside to get in my party. All my guests had V.I. P. entrance passes so they wouldn't have to wait in line. When we got in it was just as crowded, but surprisingly you had room to mingle. Everyone had a champagne bottle in hand. The D.J. gave me a shot out over the speakers, as I made my way to tables greeting my guests. My family was seated at one table, friends and associates at others. I said hello to my mom and dad who wished me Happy Birthday and complemented my party. I saw my little brother there too. I asked my pop how he got in. He told me he had put dye over his beard and rode in the car with my uncle. To be honest he did look grown with the beard, plus he had the height to go with it, so I guess he fit right in. He yelled out "Happy birthday!" while he was dancing with some big butt girl who could have been his mother. I even seen my aunt Cookie. "Who in the hell brought her?" I thought.

See Cookie was one of those relatives you only see at family cook outs. She was about 50 years old, 5 feet tall, about 160 pounds, and was loud and obnoxious. She could out drink the best drunk on earth. For her to be so short she had some big saggy breasts. She was a mess, in a purple pant suit on with this gold sheer wrap around scarf, and black and gold heels. A sight to behold. She always kept a box cutter on her person too. She was an old gansta bitch.

Nevertheless, she knew how to have a good time when she wasn't busy arguing. Tonight I gave her the benefit of the doubt. I passed by my crew and said what up to them and thanked them for coming through.

To my surprise I see Carlos sitting at a table. He wasn't in V.I.P. He opted for a small table in the back looking inconspicuous. He really didn't like crowds so I understood why he chose not to sit in V.I.P. He really wasn't dressed too fancy. Just a grey suit and some loafers. Real mellow. He then whispered to me, I hope you're ready in three days, because it's on again." I nodded my head, "Yup!" I was ready indeed. He handed me an envelope, and said "Happy birthday." I opened it and found $1000 in cash.

Million Dollar Dream
Derrick Felder

The music was jamming and everybody was grooving, having a good time. I danced to every song and was on my second bottle of champagne. I was feeling quite tipsy. I danced with Ashley, Tasha, and my mom that night. My 'lil brother was trying to crack on every girl he saw. His fake beard was starting to run down his cheek, but he didn't seem to let it affect him. Raddic was doing his two step with Ashley. It was great. My old head was enjoying himself.

Out of the blue I spotted my other old head by the bar. I knew him from the projects out on Roberts Ave. We met eyes as I walked to him. We embraced with a manly hug. I told I didn't expect him to be there, but it was good seeing him. He really didn't go out. He stayed low key every day, just like he had taught me.

I heard rumors that he had millions from the late 80's, but no one knew for sure. He trusted no one, so nobody really knew anything about him. Come to think about it, I didn't even know his name. I guess that's why he was a survivor in the game. I called him old head all my life.

The nigga was sort of like a ghost or a mystery man, on some Keiser Sosa shit. As I was talking, some woman patted me on my shoulder for a dance. I told her I'd be right with her. When I turned around my old head had disappeared. Just like that he was gone, leaving a birthday envelope with $800 in it. I scanned the entire bar for him, but came up empty. "Hey thanks anyway old head." I said to myself.

The party carried on for hours. We did the soul train line, old school dances, and we coupled danced. I was sweating up my suit and the liquor began to take over. I took off my jacket and started swinging it over my head while dancing on top of a table. The crowd was cheering me on. Suddenly I noticed Gunter in the corner of my eye. My aunt Cookie was cussing him out. I walked up to try and calm the situation, but she kept on going. Gunter was shook as hell. I don't even know what provoked the argument, but I would bet money on it that Cookie was the culprit. That Henny had her tripping. I saw her reaching in her purse for her box cutter, my eyes widened as I looked at the D.J., praying that he did something. He caught my signal and saved the night by playing my aunt's favorite song: The Electric Slide. And just like that, she snapped out of her raging trance and started sliding. One by one everyone joined in until it became a group activity.

All the older guests broke to the dance floor, while the younger ones clapped along and laughed. Cookie was breaking it down. She was dancing so hard that one of her flabby titties popped out of her blouse. Everyone turned their face in disgust, while she calmly put it back in her shirt. It didn't bother me. That would happen at every cook out she attended. It's like her old ass titties had a mind of their own.

I was on my fourth bottle of Christal, and I was drunk as a skunk. Tasha had put all of my birthday cards in her purse. Just then a cart on wheels came rolling out with a huge cake on it. Tasha kissed me on my lips and said, "Happy Birthday Russ." Everyone gathered around to sing Happy Birthday to me. Everybody I knew was there. It was beautiful. My seventeenth birthday was one to remember.

Chapter 24

I awoke to the ultimate headache. All that drinking last night had me feeling like pure shit. When I awoke I found myself on the living room sofa, fully dressed. I don't even recall how I got home. There was a note attached to the refrigerator. I didn't even feel like going to get it.

I staggered to the kitchen and snatched the note off of the frig', and took it back to the sofa. I had to sit down because I still felt drunk and my stomach was extra queasy. There were two Advils on the coffee table along with a glass of water. I popped the pills and sat back to read the letter. It was from Tasha.

Dear Russell,

By the time you read this letter I'll be at work. I took the car, but don't worry I'm only taking a half day. I didn't want to wake you. You had way too much to drink last night, if you remember. You passed out in the limo on the way home. I put your money in the bedroom you were throwing it in the air at the party. Yeah, you were doing some total nut shit. I forgive you. It was the alcohol.

Your friend Raddic helped me take you in the house. He left with Ashley afterwards. I left a jug of apple juice and ginger ale in the kitchen. There's Advil in the medicine cabinet. I'll be home by 1:00.

Love,

Tasha xoxoxoxoxo

I left the note on the table, then went to the refrigerator to get some ginger ale. I filled the tallest glass I could find. I stripped down to my boxers and crawled back on the sofa and went back to sleep. When I woke back up it was 2:00 and Tasha was already home from work. She had ran me a bath and was making me some scrambled eggs. I said hi to her before making my way to the bathroom.

The warm water made me feel a little better. I wasn't really drunk anymore, but I still had a slight headache. I wondered how much money I made for my party. I almost forgot that I was charging $25 at the door, well except for my guests. I also wanted to know what lady won the mean shoe contest. I asked Tasha, "Hey Tasha, come here." She came walking in the bathroom from the kitchen.

"Your food is on the table when you get out."

"Thanks....Ay who collected all the door money?"

"I did silly. You made like $12,000 plus all the money you got in gifts from people. I put it in the bedroom."

"That's why I love you girl. Who won the mean shoe contest?"

"Some hoochie looking heifer with damn near no clothes on. Her shoes were nice though. I think Vera Wang stilettoes."

After I got out of the tub, I dried off in the bedroom where I could count my money. I had $19,000 when I entered the party, plus $12,000 from the door and another $7,000 in gifts. Not bad. I almost made my money back that I kicked out for the party. I got dressed, ate breakfast, took a shit (you know eggs clean my system right out.) then headed out the door. I had running around to do.

When I got in my car I instantly turned some slow jams on. My head wasn't in the mood for no hard rap shit. I drove out to Ashley's house to see if she'd go check out the house in Conshohocken. I didn't bother calling, I just drove over there. When I got there of course she wasn't there, so I called her on her cell phone. She picked up on the third ring. "Hello." she answered.

"Yo Ash... where you at?"

"Well, I'm over Raddic's. I stayed here last night."

"Get him to drop you off. I'm in front of your house. I need to go look at that house I wanted to get."

"Aight… I was on my way home anyway."

"Tell Raddic I said what up."

While I was waiting for Ashley, I remembered what Carlos said about being ready in three days ... Well two days now. I had to get the limo ready and inform Ash. I called Alli Babba's and booked a hummer again, just a different color. I also wanted to check on my crew and round up some paper. Twenty minutes had went by when I seen Raddic pulling up with my cousin. They got out and Ashley ran in the house for a minute. "Hurry up Ashley. We gotta roll!" I said to her as she went in the house.

"What up Raddic?"

"Ain't shit baby. You a crazy nigga! You was cuttin' up last night."

"Yeah I heard. Where you headed?"

"I gotta go down my projects and check my youngin's out."

"Yeah I gotta go take care of a few things myself. Tell my 'lil homies I said I got mad love for them."

"Aight baby, I'm out. Tell Ashley I had to go."

"Tell her yourself. Here she comes now." Ashley was coming out her house with her pocket book in hand. Raddic gave her a hug before he sped off down North.

Me and Ash went to Conshohocken. We spent like two hours looking over the home. Ashley filled out the necessary paperwork and we were told that we would receive a call if we got approved. I was pretty confident we would. "Take this ride with me Ash. I got to go check on my crew." "Let's go." she said.

I called L. and told him to round up whatever money that they had on them. When I pulled up in front of the movie theatre, L. was waiting with a bag in his hand.

"What up L?" I said as he handed me the bag through the car window.

"How much is in here?" I asked.

"It's like $13,000 Russ."

"Good looking L. Yo swing past my apartment tonight and pick up tomorrows work. I ain't coming out tomorrow. I gotta catch up on my rest."

"Yeah I bet. You was acting up last night baby."

"Yeah you like the third person that told me. Don't forget L. Tonight come through."

As we headed back to Ashley's house, I pulled off the five grand I owed her and explained that I needed her the day after tomorrow to make that trip again. Ashley was with whatever. The money was too good for her. I came through with all my promises anyway.

I dropped her off and headed to my stash house to pick up the weed for my crew and to get Carlos' money together for the trip. I stopped past my mom's house to check on my brother. He was standing on the porch doing push-ups. I rolled up and told him to get in the car. "What up 'lil bro?"

"Ain't nuttin' Russ. Yo you was wildin' out last night."

"Me? What about your young ass all up in the club with dye on ya face looking like a bank robber? Nah you was wildin'."

"Hey man, I was doing me. I got plenty of numbers last night. Them chicks were like 28 years old!"

"That's what's up! Look I'm about to roll. Take this money to mom, and you keep this for school shopping." I pulled out a whack and gave him $2,000 for school and $3,000 to give my mom.

"Damn Russ! You a trillionaire?" I started laughing "Nah not quite. I gotta go." I gave him a pound before he headed in the house with the money. I made my way to Carlos' lot to drop off his paper.

Chapter 25

When I got in the house Tasha was on the phone with Ashley. She got off the horn five minutes after I got in. I was feeling much better since I'd ran my errands today. I still decided to lay up tomorrow. Me and Tash sat in the living room playing monopoly and sipping apple juice all night until L. stopped by around 11:30. He called me from outside, so I met him down the block where my car was parked. I passed off the weed and he gave me the remaining $12,000 he owed for the day. Before I went back to the crib, I told him to call me when he was done or if an emergency occurred.

Tasha and I finished our game, which lasted until like two in the morning. We were so tired afterwards that we fell asleep on the sofa. The next day was relaxation day for me and baby. I turned off every ringer in the house even my cell phone. I did leave my pager on in case of emergencies from my crew. We laid in bed sleeping all morning and afternoon. Later I ordered pizza as Tasha and I watched gangsta D.V.D's like Scarface, Heat, Goodfellas, and Godfather. We watched the classics, all day & night. It felt good to lay up with my main squeeze for one uninterrupted day.

Chapter 26

My beeper was vibrating on my end table when I woke up to look at it. Oh shit, it was Ashley. I called her right back. "Ash It's me."

"Damn nigga what you turned your phone off?"

"Yeah, I forgot all about this morning. What time is it?"

"It's 8:30am. We still on for today right?"

"Yeah, let me call the limo service and I'll be by to pick you right up." I called Alli Babba's and told them I would be coming by in an hour, then I went and picked Ashley up. I told her it would be the same routine as last time. Same key, same garage number, and the same amount of crates to be picked up. I gave her some money and told her to call me once she got there again. After that quick pep talk, she was headed to Miami Florida once again.

Business was really starting to pick up. We were now doing $30,000 a day and I met a guy named Cholly from Chester who was willing to pay $1,300 a pound to take to his University out West Chester. I was going to talk to Carlos about picking up more, or perhaps making two trips pcr month. More opportunities were opening and I wanted to capitalize on them. I hung out with my crew for the whole day and watched them grind.

I felt like being around them today, so I chilled with them. They really did run a tight shift. Everything was being ran the way I had it mapped. My other young boys, Mike, Ron, and Steve told me about their little episode last night at the hotel with the strippers. They had a ball. Mike got some pussy for the first time in his life. If I would've known sooner, I would've set that up way earlier.

Tonight I wasn't going home. We would repeat the hotel scene. This time in full crew mode. I called Tasha and told her not to wait up for me tonight.

Back at the Holiday Inn, we were twelve deep in two adjoining rooms with thirteen bad strippers down for whatever. My conscious was eating away at me about fucking one of these chicks, so I decided not to. All I needed was to bring something home to Tasha and my unborn seed. I settled for a couple of lap dances.

Anyway it was all about my niggaz tonight. I was tripping off 'lil Mike. This nigga was running around the room with just his boxers on tryna fuck every girl in sight. The white boy Gunter was running wild smacking bitches on the ass. This muthafucka was so pale, he looked like a fucking ghost running around butt naked. The shit was mad funny. One of the girls had the softest ass on planet earth. I decided to lay my head on it and go to sleep. At 2:00am Ashley called to tell me she made it safely and would be back tomorrow night. I told her to be safe and went back to sleep on "Ms. Booty-licious".

The following morning I left the telly early to drop Tasha off at work. When I got back I decided to take a morning run to clear my head. I picked a track out Bala Cynwyd. While I was on my third lap I spotted someone watching me from inside their car. I picked up and got the fuck out of there. I didn't have my hammer on me either. For some reason I've been feeling followed lately, but shook it off as paranoia.

114

I was headed to my stash house to drop off money and grab work when the lady from the Conshohocken house called looking for Ashley. I took the message instead. "I'm very sorry, but Ms. Wade was denied. It seems her credit history isn't that established and...." I hung up on the bitch. I was pissed now. I really wanted to surprise Tasha with that house. I wasn't giving up that easy though.

After I picked up and dropped off what was needed at the stash house, I contacted L. to pick up the days product, then headed down North Philly. I needed a personal favor from 'lil Pooh. I caught 'lil Pooh pulling his car out of a gas station when I blew my horn at him and directed him to pull over. We got out of our cars and began talking.

"How's it going Russ ... what brings you down these parts?"

"Actually I was hoping to run into you. I lucked up!"

"Well what's up? By the way, I heard about your party. NICE!"

"Yeah well it's back to work now. I need you to do a ride out Conshohocken with me. I got a job for you."

Pooh parked his car and hopped in mine. I took notice that he was dressed pretty conservatively, with some slacks and a button up shirt. "Why are you so dressed up Pooh?"

"In my line of work Russ you should never want to fit the stereo type. By day I'm quiet and gentleman-like, but by night you better get ya kids off the streets and clear the corners 'cause I'm coming."

"I feel you dog, that's why I need you."

We pulled up on Radner Street in Conshohocken and sat outside the house I thought I'd be calling home. I explained to him that the lady who would've been renting us the place turned me down on renting it and I detected some other motives as to why I was turned down. So I wanted the place vacant for a while, if you know what I mean. Pooh assured me that everything would run smoothly. I drove Pooh back to the gas station on Broad and Girard where his car was parked.

"Hey Pooh. You remember how to get back out there, right?"

"Yeah. Radner Street. I got it. Don't worry." He said smiling. Pooh was so deceptive. I knew he would be a boss one day. Later that night I'm up watching the 11:00 news with Tasha. The reporter was broadcasting live. "I'm Steven Buckner reporting to you live from Radner Street in the prestigious Conshohocken section of PA, where it seems a racially motivated vandalism has taken place. It appears that a house on this quiet suburban block was spray painted with racial slurs as well as all the windows being broken in. It seems that the culprit or culprits were apart of some sort of KKK like group, because if you take a look here the words "Die nigger" and "Long live the KKK" were written over the entire home. No neighbors have seen or heard anything. The police are still looking for suspects, or any clues that could lead to the apprehension of whomever was responsible. From the looks, this was done by a pro

116

and this crime might go unsolved. Reporting live from Channel 6, I'm Steve Buckner. "

Tasha looked on in amazement. "Russ that's the same neighborhood we were looking at houses in the other day. Why would someone want to destroy such a beautiful homes? Who would want to live there now Russ?"

"Not me Tasha" I said with a sly smirk.

Chapter 27

2:30 in the morning and I was on the phone with Ashley. She had gotten back safe and I was on my way to her house to meet her. I arrived at her house twenty minutes later and me and the limo driver went to work hauling all four crates into my wagon. I tipped the driver before sending him on his way. I turned to Ashley. "Hey Ash you feel like going to get some breakfast with me? I know an all-night diner close by."

"Sure Russ. I haven't eaten all day."

"Aight. Let me drop this stuff off and I'll be right back."

"Aight hurry up. It's late and I'm kind of tired."

I jetted to the stash house in record time to unload the crates. Once I was in the house, I counted my money again. I still had over a million dollar, but once I ran through what I had, I'd be close to two. I'd gotten so caught up in the moment that I almost forgot Ashley was waiting for me.

I drove back to her house and honked my horn for her. When she didn't answer I decided to ring her bell. Still no answer. I thought it was strange of her not to answer, since she knew I was coming back. I immediately figured she was asleep. Probably tired from the long ride. I went to the diner alone, then headed home.

I woke up around 8:30a.m. Tasha had already left for work and had taken my car, so I was stuck in the house. My house phone was now ringing, so I got out of the bed to answer it. "Hello." "You have a collect call from ...."

Chapter 28

"Yo today is popping dog, and it's still mad early." Gunter said to his soldiers. It was an exceptionally good fucking morning. Cars were lined up like crazy to get weed.

The strip was jumping. Everybody was occupied exchanging bills and grinding hard. So occupied that no one noticed the four black Crown Victorias speeding through the parking lot.

Chapter 29

"You have a collect call from.... (pause)... Ashley
...press 5 to accept the call. Hang up to decline the call." is
what the automated voice service said. I wasn't sure if I was
hearing this right, but I was sure the voice said Ashley so I
pressed 5. Ashley was absolutely hysterical. She was
crying uncontrollably and trying to talk at the same time. I
had to tell her to calm down so I could figure out what in
the hell was going on. "Ashley calm down babe and tell me
what happened."

"I don't know Russ. All I know is that I was waiting
for you to come back last night when my door was kicked
in by like ten DEA agents, waving guns, ordering me to lay
down. They hand cuffed me and brought me downtown.
Russ I'm scared."

"Ash don't panic. How did you know they were
DEA?"

"It said it on their jackets."

"Alright. Did you tell them anything?"

"No."

"Good. Sit tight, I'm sending someone down to get
you, 'cause Tasha took my car to work. Just hold tight."

I immediately called L. as soon as I hung up with
Ashley. I got no answer. I pressed redial. Still no answer.
"Shit. What the fuck is going on? Where is L?" Just then, I
hear a commotion outside. I go to the window and see my
apartment being surrounded by unmarked police cars.

I'm startled by a sudden knock at the door. "BOOM, BOOM, BOOM. Open up its DEA." I must've took too long to respond, because my door was instantly kicked off the hinges. All I saw was five foot nine officers waving Glock forties in my face.

"GET THE FUCK DOWN MUTHERFUCKER NOW!" one of the officers yelled. I placed my hands behind my head and let them take me in. When they took me down town to the station, I was immediately shoved into a room with only a long table and fold up chairs. I thought, this must be the interrogation room. I was placed in a chair followed by two officers. One took a seat while the other began talking.

"Well, well, Mr. Wade. We finally got your ass. You're going away for a long, long time. We picked up your little girlfriend Ashley last night and she told us everything, so why don't you come clean?" Then it was my turn.

"First off I don't know who or what you all are talking about, and I don't think you do either. If you did you wouldn't need me to tell you anything. Plus did you know I'm only 17? Oh don't look surprised. That's right I'm only 17, and I get more money than you get donuts buddy, so what that means is I'm a minor and what you're doing right now is 100% ILLEGAL. I know my rights. I'll be out and back to school before you can say CHEESE mutha fucka. So take these tight ass cuffs and stick 'em up ya ass!"

The detective became furious. He got right up in my face. So close I could smell his bad breath.

"Okay smart ass. Special Agent Sanchez, will you please explain to this cock sucking piece of drug dealing shit why he'll be staying with us for a while."

A third officer came through the door. I wasn't expecting this face to show up. Not in a million years. At that moment I thought I was better off dead.

Chapter 30

Tasha was at work. She took pride in her job as a hostess. She should've been 'cause she was good at it. Everyone loved her, especially the regular customers. She remembered everyone on a first name basis. I mean everyone knew Tasha. Even on her days off the people would ask about her. For her to be working there such a short period of time, she was respected like a seasoned veteran.

It was 12:00pm and Tasha hadn't taken her lunch break yet. The manager had to force her to take a break.

"Tasha, please take a break girl. You're gonna have a stroke around here."

"Alright Mr. Charlie."

Tasha decided to hang out at the restaurant's bar which had two TV's. One had the news on as she watched a replay of the events that took place outside of a movie theatre's parking lot in the Northeast. What she saw was L, Gunter, and Jeremy along with a few others being placed in patty wagons. Even though their faces were being blurred out on TV, because they were juveniles, she knew exactly who they were. It was straight pandemonium out there with cars and people racing off the scene like crazy. Tasha covered her mouth with her hand in shock, as she raced to the pay phone to contact Russ. He never answered.

Chapter 31

... Special Agent Sanchez came walking through the door and I swear, I could feel all the strength, blood and energy being drained from my body. My head began spinning, my legs grew limp, and my mouth became as dry as the Sahara Desert. I looked up at the man who was known as Special Agent Sanchez. I knew him better as Carlos.

Chapter 32

(Tasha)

I automatically assumed the worst when the phone went unanswered. In a heat of panic I ran to my manager with tears in my eyes and explained to him what I seen on the news and how I thought that Russ might somehow be in trouble with the guy on TV.

"Tasha-Tasha, calm down sweetheart. Why don't you take the rest of the day off and contact his parents." Mr. Charlie said. I clocked out and headed home, not having the slightest clue what to do or who to call. I definitely couldn't call his parents. Maybe Ashley could help if something was wrong. I decided not to jump to conclusions. Maybe he just wasn't answering the phone.

When I finally arrived in front of my apartment, all my fears were confirmed as neighbors were outside telling me all that went down this morning and how the cops dragged Russ out of the apartment. When I finally got inside, the place was trashed like someone was looking for something. Shit was everywhere. I wanted to straighten up, but didn't quite know where to start. In the kitchen I noticed that the refrigerator door was left open, so I figured I would start there. "What in the hell could the police possibly be looking for here?" I said as I expressed my anger out loud. At the bottom of the refrigerator I took notice of a piece broken, which sort of caused it to stick out like a flap. I bent down to try and fix it or try to see what damage was done. I spotted a shoe box behind the flap.

I pulled the flap all the way off. It definitely was a shoe box. I decided to open it. The contents inside the box had me suddenly nervous. It was a large hand gun and piles of money stacked underneath, I couldn't possibly pretend to be that naive, as to act like I didn't know where my boyfriend's money came from. That still didn't stop me from breaking down right there on the kitchen floor. I couldn't help it. All I know is drug dealers seemed to get put away for a long time.   I had no other logical rationale as to why my boyfriend had the type of money he had.

We lived better than most adults did, for our age. I just wondered why Russ kept so much from me. Nevertheless he treated me good and I know he would be the perfect father. So I wiped my tears away and waited for someone to call with an explanation. I put the money and the gun back where I found it and sat in the living room. I had to be strong for my man.

Chapter 33

(Russ)

I was staring up at the guy who I once knew as Carlos, now Special Agent Sanchez. I couldn't believe this was happening. Carlos couldn't be the police. He just couldn't. Carlos began talking. Everything went right in one ear and out the other. "Listen Russ. I know you don't wanna hear anything I have to say, but right now you've been indicted by a federal grand jury for possession with the intent to distribute one ton of marijuana.

All your friends have been charged and so has Ashley. Be smart kid and help yourself. I know you're an intelligent kid. You don't want to be the first kid doing 20 years on a major marijuana indictment. Do you?"

"Let me explain something to you Special Agent Carlos, or whatever you call yourself. Ya see I'm cut from a totally different fabric than most young cats. You're absolutely correct, I am intelligent. That's why I'm smart enough to know not to fuck with the same snake twice. Before I turn bad, I'd rather die in prison. Besides I'm innocent. Now where's my lawyer?"

"Okay Russell. Have it your way." Agent Sanchez said.

Deep down inside I was scared shitless. I've been in trouble before, but never like this. I also knew it was a possibility that I might get booked. A very good possibility. I'd bought from an agent.

After the brief interrogation, I was processed and charged as an adult and detained at a detention center in downtown Philadelphia. When the U.S. Marshals brought me there, I was stripped, searched, and issued a 2X orange jump suit. I was then taken to a wall where my picture could be taken. After which, I was given a health examination and then placed in a temporary holding cell where I would await block designation.

While I was waiting, I took notice that the other inmates had on green jump suits rather than orange. My nosy ass had to ask one of the guards what was so special about me.

"Yo guard.... Over here." I said. The guard came walking over to my door and said, "What is it?"

"Yo, why do I have this orange jumpsuit and don't nobody else?"

"Because you're going to a Special Housing Unit."

"What the hell does that mean?"

"It means you're going to the hole."

"For what?"

"I have no idea kid Let me get back to work."

I sat back on the cold bench in the holding cell and waited to be called. I just wanted to talk to someone normal. An hour later my name was called to be moved.

Another guard appeared and gave me my new identification card, as he took me through a door and onto an elevator where I was told to face the back wall.   I was being taken up eight floors to the Special Housing Unit. Again I was stripped searched, then given a T- shirt, pair of socks, pair of boxers, pillow case, two sheets, a blanket, and a pillow. I was then escorted down the corridor to cell 814. While I was being taken to my cell, I asked the guard why I was being placed in Special Housing Unit. He told me due to my age the Warden thought I'd be safer here, even though I was being charged as an adult. When I asked to make a phone call he informed me that all phone numbers had to be approved by the jail. He then gave me a phone form to fill out. I completed it right there using the officers pen and handed it back to him. This guard seemed to be pretty cool, so I filled out a special visitation form to have my girl come up.

I needed to see Tasha bad. I had a lot of explaining to do and I needed her to take care of some things regarding this fucked up situation. After that ordeal I was finally locked in my cell and given a bagged lunch. I was in no mood for eating, so I just laid down on the hard ass bed and left the bag on the floor.

The following morning I was notified of my approval of the phone list and visitation privileges. I also received a pin number to activate my phone. As soon as I got the chance I called Tasha. (ring-ring-ring)

"Hello." Tasha answered. The automated voice picked up. "This a collect call from a federal prison ... you will be charged $1.50 for this call. This call is from Russell. Press 5 to accept the call. Hang up to decline the call." The call was accepted.

"Hello." I said.

"Yeah it's me Russ. Are you okay?"

"Yeah baby I'm fine. Look I don't wanna talk on these phones, so listen. Come to 7th and Arch Street to the federal detention center today. I can have visits. Come now."

"I got it baby. I'll be there. Don't worry, we're in this together. I love you Russell."

"I love you too Tasha. See you when you get here. Bye."

When I returned to my cell I was so anxious to see Tasha, I couldn't stop pacing. When I finally settled down it was chow time. Lunch was being served.   They pushed a brown tray through a metal opening in my door. When I looked down at what was supposed to be lunch, I felt the urge to push it back out at the officer. Instead I took a deep breath and dealt with it. I had to eat something. I took another deep breath and remembered I had a bagged lunch the day before, that I didn't eat. I opened the bag, which contained a turkey sandwich and some cookies. I settled for that instead.

Thirty minutes later the guard was   calling my name for legal mail and a visit. I took the mail and opened it. It stated that I was scheduled for court tomorrow to be federally arraigned on charges. I had no idea of what to make of my situation. I guess I'd have to wait and see. Right now I had a visit to tend to.

"Wade....You ready?"

"Yes sir." I replied to the guard. I was escorted out of my cell and down the hall to the visiting quarters. I was placed in a room where Tasha was waiting in a blue chair behind a glass window. One phone was on each side of the glass. I picked up.   "Hey Tash. I'm glad you made it down so fast."

"Baby what's going on?" I've been worried sick about you. Are you okay?"

"Yeah Tash, I'm fine. These muthafuckas are trying to set me up, but I'm gonna beat these charges. You watch."

"Baby I'm scared. You were on the news along with Ashley and your other friends. The police said it was one of the biggest operations in Northeast history Your mom called the apartment crying. She's obviously aware of everything that's going on and, your father wants to know what he can do to help. Oh by the way, I found some money and a gun under the refrigerator, what should I do?"

"First thing, tell my parents to just sit tight until I hear something. In the mean time I need for you to take ten grand of that money and get me a lawyer retained. I gotta go to court tomorrow so step on it too. It's this lawyer named Guy I've been hearing a lot about, he's supposed to be good with drug cases. His office is on 100 S. Broad St. See if he'll take the case I used up my only phone call today, so if he shows tomorrow then I know everything is cool on that part I'm scheduled for court tomorrow."

"Russell, do you need me at your hearing?"

"Nah, from what I heard and read, it's only an arraignment. I'll go have my charges read and decide how I'm pleading. Also take an extra ten grand for Ashley. See if he can recommend somebody to represent her. If she calls tell her don't worry about nothing. Everything's gonna work out fine."

"Russ, I did talk to Ashley. They're holding her here too. She sounded pretty alright on the phone, but I know this place is killing her. You gotta get her outta here. She

131

told me I could use her car since they didn't confiscate it. The keys are in her house. I'll go pick them up on my way from here."

"Yeah, take her car, I don't want you driving my wagon anyway, just in case they wanna impound it. Don't worry Tash, I'm going to beat this shit. I don't need you worrying about me. Once you take care of the lawyer, I want you to start back at work and think about those correspondence courses for school alright. You're carrying our baby, so take it easy. One more thing. Take $500, go to the post office, get a money order, and mail it to me here."

"Alright Russ."

"Wade- your visiting time is up." The guard yelled.

"Aight Tash, I'll call you when I can. I love you."

"I love you too baby."

I blew a kiss at Tasha before I was taken back to my cell. When I got back to my cell door, I looked in and seen someone. "Just what the fuck I didn't need." I said. They'd given me a fucking celly to make matters worse.

I stepped in the cell with the ice grill on my face. This guy looked at me and extended his hand for me to shake it. "What's going on? My names Lij, from Lancaster." I ignored his polite gesture and said "Look Lij from Lancaster, I ain't in the mood to be meeting no new friends, so let me do me and you do you." I walked away from him and looked out the small window we had in the cell. The window overlooked the downtown city. It reminded me of the view at the Hyatt hotel. I was really stressing now.

Chapter 34

My celly Lij had woke me up for breakfast the following morning. I was kind of glad 'cause I wanted to be already awake when they called me for court. I felt kind of bad for being so rude to Lij the day before, so I decided to thank him for waking me up to eat. We sat there and ate and talked a little bit before they called me for court.

The nigga Lij was actually cool. He was seventeen like me and had got caught selling weed too. Oh yeah, and was a part of the most major fraud indictments on the East Coast. We actually had a lot in common. We were the same age, same complexion, and both had the ambition to get that paper, despite how young we were.

"Wade…. Court." the officer yelled into the cell.

"Yo….Good luck down there man. " Lij said.

"Thanks." I said. I was gonna need it.

When I arrived in the court room I noticed my attorney present along with Ashley handcuffed and shackled next to her lawyer. I felt bad for getting her involved. She had a promising future as a lawyer, now she was the one in need of legal counsel. The judge read off the list of charges and asked did we understand. We both agreed to our charges as far as what they meant. Then we both entered not guilty pleas. My conscious was getting the best of me, so I tapped my lawyer and told him to relay a message to Ashley and her lawyer. I wanted him to tell Ashley to think about testifying against me in exchange for the dismissal of her   charges.

I looked over as my attorney relayed the message. What I got was a middle finger from Ashley as she mouthed the word N-E-V-E-R. I guess it was settled. We were going to trial. The judge set a date 90 days from today.

Chapter 35

The next two and a half months went by like a blur. All the while Tasha stood right by me. She came to visit me every week and handled all the affairs with me and Ashley's attorneys. I also told her where the key to my stash house was and to only go to it at night and with my permission only.

Tasha was also doing well with her correspondence courses to receive her diploma. Her pregnancy was going well. She had decided to contact my mother for advice. My mother got her to go to a clinic that dealt with teenage pregnancy and how to cope with it. They also offered a lamas class. Besides my situation, everything was cool.

Trial was scheduled for next week and my attorney was asking for the balance of his fees. Ashley's lawyer was too. Together I needed $40,000. I spoke to Tasha about it A.S.A.P and she got right on it. I figured I was all set. Four days before trial I got an unexpected visit from Tasha. I was in the middle of playing a game of casino (a jail house card game) with Lij, when I was called to a visit. I was getting my ass kicked anyway so I ain't mind rolling out on him. When I got to the visiting room I noticed Tasha was crying, so I immediately picked up the phone.

"Tash…. What's the matter?" I asked.

"It's the money Russ ... It's the goddamn money. IT'S GONE!"

The words just echoed in my brain a thousand times "Gone...gone ... gone... gone. ...GONE ... GONE!"

I calmed down and asked, "Tasha what do you mean gone? What the fuck happened?"

"I went there like you said. The lock was cut off, so I went in. The house was totally empty, so I ran out and got back in the car and drove off."

In a fit of rage I jumped up, and started banging the phone against the window until the guards came and escorted me out. Tasha just stood there all alone, helplessly crying. It was all my fault. Everything I ever loved got destroyed as a result of this life style I chose.

I went back to my cell and cried my eyes out. I didn't even give a fuck if my celly heard me. All I could think about was my family and how I hurt them and let them down. T., someone who I considered a friend, who I shot cold bloodedly for nothing, and now Tasha, the only girl I've ever truly cared about, who was now 6 months pregnant with our child, I was leaving her out there to face this world alone. I felt worse than shit. If I would've known this was the price for stardom, I would've gladly settled for mediocrity. Instead I was left to face the music. Like Jigga said before, "Gotta Learn To Live With Regrets."

Chapter 36

Trial Day

Today was the big dance. Me and Ashley against the United States of America. What the fuck did we ever do to the whole America? Our jury consisted of three blacks, and nine whites. All of them old enough to be our grandparents. So much for a jury of our peers, I thought.

We had selected them the day before. They were the best picks of the litter. I knew we were doomed. Ashley and I were appointed federal defenders who knew very little about our case. Nevertheless, they were there. The federal defender told me that the judge might grant us a week extension to review the particulars of the case. I told him not to bother. What good would a lousy week do. The courtroom was packed with family and community support along with Tasha, who looked tired and worn out from crying night after night. I was scared to death knowing I was facing more time than I had on earth. I looked over at Ashley who had the same look of fear on her face.

The Honorable Judge Kane came in and everybody rose to stand. After all the bullshit, the prosecution started with their opening arguments. They already had a picture painted that I was a menace to society and that I was arrested before for similar offences, and I didn't learn my lesson. He went on and on and on.

The jury looked at us like we were murderers. Our bum ass attorneys said nothing except that we were good kids. What kind of opening argument was that, I thought. Both sides went back and forth for about an hour. The prosecution brought in Special Agent Sanchez, who testified to how long he worked for the DEA, which was 15 years and how he orchestrated the deal to sell me one thousand pounds of marijuana on two different occasions along with a .40 caliber hand gun, and how Ashley was the runner. I wondered how he knew that being as though he never met her on any occasion. Just then a video recorder and screen were brought into the courtroom. The lights were dimmed, and what appeared on the screen was Ashley and the employee at the storage company loading the crates onto some sort of flatbed on wheels. Once the tape was finished I knew we were in for it. Somehow there was a tape inside the garage waiting to record anyone who picked up the crates.

Our lawyers rebutted the prosecutions attack by pointing out that Ashley had no knowledge of marijuana being in those crates and besides the testimony of officer Sanchez saying I was the leader, there was no other proof to support that. I wasn't on any tapes and most importantly there were no drugs or money found. Period. Let alone on our possession. I thought to myself that without any physical evidence, we stood a good chance.

Chapter 37

It took the jury all of twenty minutes to deliberate and come back with two guilty verdicts. My knees began to buckle as I looked back at my family and Tasha. I glanced over at Ashley. She returned my look with a blank glare of her own.

"We the jury find the defendant Ashley Wade GUILTY on all counts."

The audience broke down with shouts of injustice. The judge banged her gavel for order.

"We the jury find the defendant Russell Wade GUILTY on all counts."

The court was in an uproar. The judge banged her gavel again and said. "This court is adjourned. Please remove the prisoners."

We were rushed out of the courtroom so fast I couldn't even curse out my attorney. I did catch a glimpse of Tasha who was holding her stomach and crying with her head down. I was speechless all the way back to my cell. All I could think about was Tasha, Tasha, Tasha.

I knew I would be summoned to a sentencing hearing soon. I didn't want anyone to be there for that. It would be too painful. When I got back to my cell, Lij was standing up staring out of the window looking down at the streets. I jumped on my bed and stared at the ceiling.

"How did you make out Russ?" Lij said.

"We got found guilty dog."

"Sorry to hear that."

"Yeah so am I."

I kept silent while Lij gazed out the window. Something must've really had his attention out there.

"Yo Russ, come look out here. Look at this chick tripping in the middle of the damn street."

"Lij, I really don't feel like it dog. Not right now."

"Nah man look, she's really buggin'."

Reluctantly, I got up to see what the big fuss was about.

"Oh my god no!" It was Tasha in the middle of the street on her knees with her hands in the air like she was asking God why.

Even though we were eight floors up, I knew my Tasha from anywhere, plus her protruding belly gave her up. I was wondering what she was doing as tears began to swell up in my eyes. I started banging on the window telling her to get up. She seemed oblivious to her surroundings as traffic began to back up because of her.

"Where were my parents?" I thought. She continued to cry hysterically as she reached into her purse which was on the ground as well, and pulled out my .40 caliber hand gun. I began panicking.

"Tasha No!" I continued banging even though I knew no one could hear. I then began screaming for the guards. No one seemed to be paying me any attention. I watched Tasha place the barrel to the side of her temple. Now I was screaming like crazy. "Tasha…. Baby no! Tasha no! Somebody help! Tasha NOOO!" She looked up to the sky and pulled the trigger. BOOM!

140

Chapter 38

When I awoke I was drenched in sweat. I didn't have on a prison jumpsuit though. I had on a Mischino Hoody and jeans. I was in my 3rd period history class. I awoke from my dream so abruptly that my teacher allowed me to excuse myself from the classroom. I wiped my face, grabbed my book bag, and left.

While I was walking the halls I checked my bag. I still had two ounces in there intended for L. Just then I spotted Jeremy walking in my direction so I approached him. "Hey you seen L. today?"

"Nah Russ I ain't seen him. You alright? You look shook up?"

"Yeah I'm cool. Here take these, I'm leaving school early. I'm just feeling a little funny today that's all. If you see L. tell him to page me."   I passed off the weed and left school.

When I stepped out in front of Northeast High, I felt relieved. The fresh air did me justice.

"Man…Fuck a day dream. That was a day nightmare." I said out loud. I was just happy it was over, plus I was starving. I made my way over to Burger King. Inside, the line was pretty long so I took a seat at a nearby booth with a window view looking out at the streets. I had a lot on my mind. Mainly because my dream seemed so realistic.

As I looked out the window I saw truancy officers patrolling the school grounds. I felt like my dream was some sort of forewarning. I got up and ordered a breakfast sandwich and orange juice, since the crowded line calmed down. Once my meal was bagged, I returned to my booth. I unwrapped my grub and slouched down in the seat. The only thought I had……"WHAT 'S NEXT FOR RUSSELL WADE?"

THE END

Made in the USA
Columbia, SC
03 December 2018